"You are both forthright and honest, my lady. I admire your plain, frank candor. After all my experience with dissemblers I have come across, it is refreshing to hear plain speaking. That I cannot fault."

Her eyes narrowed with suspicion at his words of praise and then she laughed. "You are chivalrous, sir. I respect that."

Her sudden and unexpected laughter was both joyous and warm. John suspected it was a long time since she had laughed at all. He suffered a slight sense of shock as, still smiling, she looked at him fully. There was something in her eyes that set his heart beating uncomfortably fast. He felt a great sense of excitement, and he could not but marvel at himself. She was a stranger to him with a mind of her own. Yet somehow he knew that beneath Catherine Stratton's exterior there was a lush sensuality. Instinctively he knew, too, that no matter how arrogant she might conceivably be, she had that magic quality that could well enslave a man and bring him to his knees.

Author Note

Writing is something I enjoy and it gives me great personal satisfaction. I enjoy reading books from all genres, but historical romance is my favorite.

Once again I have chosen to write about the English Civil War, a period that was probably one of the most turbulent times in British history. In 1648, everyone hoped the war was over. But there were two more battles to come—Dunbar in 1650 and the decisive Battle of Worcester in 1651, which saw the young King Charles II and those Royalists who escaped the battle exiled across the Channel. King Charles II was restored to his throne in 1660, on his thirtieth birthday.

Resisting Her Enemy Lord is a story that touches on the war. The upheaval and loss of this time was experienced by almost every family across the length and breadth of the kingdom. For Catherine Stratton, living in Carlton Bray Castle on the Welsh Marches, with her husband away fighting the king's cause and everyone dependent on her for protection and sustenance, she has been forced to endure more than most.

When she learns of her husband's death, she is determined to forge a new life for herself now that she's a widow—until John Stratton, the heir to Carlton Bray and colonel in the Parliamentary army, appears in her life to change everything. He has come to escort her to London, to her father's house. So begins their journey together. Both are beset with emotional conflicts that must be resolved.

HELEN DICKSON

Resisting Her
Enemy Lord

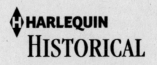
HARLEQUIN
HISTORICAL

HARLEQUIN®
HISTORICAL™

Recycling programs
for this product may
not exist in your area.

ISBN-13: 978-1-335-50604-7

Resisting Her Enemy Lord

Harlequin Enterprises ULC
22 Adelaide St. West, 40th Floor
Toronto, Ontario M5H 4E3, Canada
www.Harlequin.com

Printed in U.S.A.

Helen Dickson was born and still lives in South Yorkshire, UK, with her retired farm manager husband. Having moved out of the busy farmhouse where she raised their two sons, she now has more time to indulge in her favorite pastimes. She enjoys being outdoors, traveling, reading and music. An incurable romantic, she writes for pleasure. It was a love of history that drove her to writing historical fiction.

Books by Helen Dickson

Harlequin Historical

When Marrying a Duke...
The Devil Claims a Wife
The Master of Stonegrave Hall
Mishap Marriage
A Traitor's Touch
Caught in Scandal's Storm
Lucy Lane and the Lieutenant
Lord Lansbury's Christmas Wedding
Royalist on the Run
The Foundling Bride
Carrying the Gentleman's Secret
A Vow for an Heiress
The Governess's Scandalous Marriage
Reunited at the King's Court
Wedded for His Secret Child
Resisting Her Enemy Lord

Castonbury Park

The Housemaid's Scandalous Secret

Visit the Author Profile page
at Harlequin.com for more titles.

Chapter One

Night was drawing in and freezing cold rain and wind buffeted the small group of riders from every direction. These were desperate times. Armed bands frequently travelled the roads and in the dark it was not easy to identify friend from foe. Had the Royalists and Scots not been routed at Preston in August by Oliver Cromwell's New Model Army, and should the riders encounter such a force, they would stand to be imprisoned and either ransomed off or, at worst, suffer an ignoble death. Mercifully, good fortune had been on the side of Parliament that day and the Scots sent packing back to the border.

A small band of men rode through the village of Carlton situated in the Welsh Marches. Two horses pulled a wooden cart carrying the earthly remains of Lord Thomas Stratton. Ahead of them the huge stone structure that was Carlton Bray Castle appeared large and ominous in their sights. The brooding, medieval edifice, the massive walls and dull mullioned windows were unwelcoming, even from a distance. Colonel John Stratton sighed his relief. Built of blood and bone in the twelfth century, the castle's ancient stones were pitted and scarred from past battles.

The central keep, unapologetically bold and built foursquare in the courtyard with clean, straight lines, stretched like an arm into the sky, as though it would swoop them up and dash them against the defensible walls should they dare to venture too close. Defying entrance to the enemy and protecting those within, it towered over the sleeping village and the surrounding countryside, the small windows having seen four centuries blown past on the wind.

At last John Stratton felt a warm fire and a cup of wine was close. The half-dozen exhausted riders rattled across the drawbridge which spanned a dry ditch, the supporting timbers rotten in places with age. No one stopped them to enquire as to their business or acknowledge that the Lord of Carlton Bray Castle had come home at last. The clattering of the horses' hooves disturbed the silence as they passed beneath the raised portcullis and entered the inner bailey. Drawing rein, they dismounted. Guards, disturbed from their slumbers, appeared from the shadows, one of them mumbling something about the ungodly hour, until his eyes lit upon the coffin and he joined his fellow grooms and stepped respectfully aside before taking the horses away to the stables to be rubbed down and fed.

John shuddered, certain he could hear the whispers of days gone by, of good and bad who had resided within the walls, their tortured voices rising up from the dungeons and echoing round the castle.

From a window high in the keep, Catherine Stratton looked down on the covered casket containing her husband's dead body before passing on to the men who had escorted it from the north. The new heir of Carlton Bray Castle and estate was John Stratton, the noble Earl Fitzroy of the Sussex branch of the family. His heritage was so vast, with land and properties in both Sussex and the Midlands, that Thomas had told her there were few noblemen in England who could surpass it.

She had never met John Stratton, but in the early days of her marriage to Thomas he had told her about his handsome cousin. By his account John Stratton was the most impressive of his cousins. As a second son, with the lure of adventure strong in his veins, he had become a soldier. Colourful and exciting were the military exploits of John Stratton, the charismatic soldier with a reputation as being one for the ladies, although he was always discreet in his affairs. By Thomas's account he was arrogant and ruthless—in fact, he was everything Catherine hated. He was here now not only to see his cousin laid to rest, but to claim his inheritance. Catherine had her own ideas of what she would do with her future, and, seeing Thomas's heir for the first time, she was determined that nothing would sway her from her plans.

Shrouded in a black cloak, he stood back from the cart. She could not make out his features, but she could see he was as dark as Thomas had been fair. She felt a strange slithering unease. He had an air of command she had never encountered before—not even in her father.

As if the man sensed she was staring at him, he tilted his head back and looked up at the window where she stood. The meeting of their eyes was fleeting, but before Catherine could take stock of his features he turned away.

Ordering the castle guards to take care of his escort and hunched against the biting wind, John and his steward, Will Price, climbed the steep steps of the fortress-like entry. The massive door at the top moaned its rusty objection as it was pulled wide by a servant within. Showing deference, he stepped aside and bade them enter the lower hall of Carlton Bray Castle.

Their boots sounded hollowly on the bare boards. Tall and powerfully built, John Stratton looked as if he could claim the very ground on which he walked. He emanated an authority and forcefulness that made every man who had fought under him during the civil wars obey his command. With his gloved hand on the hilt of his sword and his sodden cloak swept back over his broad shoulders dripping water on to the floor, he paused to assess his surroundings, finding them as he remembered when he had last been here as a youth. He noted the fine chimney breast carved with the Stratton coat of arms. The cold stone walls were hung with dusty old standards and weaponry from another age. Stout wooden beams hung with cobwebs and a wide open fireplace where logs sizzled beneath the great stone arch gave out a welcoming heat. John peered up into the corners of the hall already shadowed by dusk.

Will strode to the hearth, holding his hands out to the heat. Hearing the sharp tread of boots descending the stone stairs, John stood still, waiting to see who would materialise from the deep shadows of the staircase. A figure appeared, a man, he thought, until more of the person was revealed and he saw it was a woman attired in male garb. She drew his whole attention, so at one was she with her surroundings. Beneath the padded doublet his discerning eye could see the fabric pulling over her breasts—there was nothing masculine about her form.

Seemingly wholly unconcerned with his arrival, she paused, studying him with cool interest, her expression immobile and guarded with as little of alarm in it as it had of proud self-assertion. She was tall, as slender as a willow, her hair caught in a band at the nape of her neck, the vibrant tresses the colour of antique gold, curling down her spine. Her skin was creamy, glowing, a soft flush highlighting perfect cheekbones. Her lips were moist and the shade of coral that lay on the bottom of tropical seas, her eyes as green and bright as emeralds and framed by sweeping dark lashes. Without expression her eyes swept over him, sharp, calmly assessing. Pausing on the second step, she had the advantage of height.

John strode towards her. The piercing green gaze from her eyes almost knocked him back off his feet. A spark of desire was sent coursing through his body and for a moment he was rendered speechless. If this was Lady Stratton, she could not have been more different to what he had expected. Beneath the solemn yet proud exterior he believed was a woman of surprising qualities. What irresistible charms were concealed beneath her male garb? As he felt himself undergoing the same close scrutiny he was giving her, their eyes met and he held her steady gaze. For one discomforting moment it seemed that she was staring into the very heart of him, getting the measure of him, of his faults and failings. He had never seen eyes that contained more energy and depth.

He bowed. 'My lady. Colonel John Stratton—Lord Fitzroy—at your service.' The deep timbre of his voice reverberated around the hall.

'I know who you are,' she was quick to reply. 'You are expected. You have brought Thomas home—and, I imagine, as my husband's heir, come to claim your inheritance, such as it is. I have had no account of Thomas for nigh on four years—not since the Royalist army was defeated at Marston Moor. Neither hide nor hair has been noted of him since—until I received your letter. You were with him—at the end?'

'Sadly, no, I was not. I arrived shortly after.' He indicated his companion with a movement of his head, a man tall and well-built with a shock of tawny hair. 'This is Will Price—my steward.'

'Forgive me it I do not curtsy. It would be inappropriate and laughable dressed as I am.' Her voice was well-modulated, confident and distinctly feminine. 'Welcome to Carlton Bray. I have had accommodation prepared.'

There was no smile of welcome to warm her conventional words. No look in her eyes to indicate shyness or modesty—her manner showed no sign of grief that her husband was dead. John suspected this was no ordinary young woman. He sensed in her an independent spirit, which had no room for convention or etiquette. There was nothing demure about her, unlike the young ladies who flitted in and out of his mother's circle in Sussex, whose eyes would be ingenuously cast down, even among those they knew, which was proper. This young woman showed none of the restraint instilled into girls of good family. She stared directly into his eyes. Her own glowed with an inner light and hinted of the woman hidden beneath her lovely features. For all her dignified composure and confidence, she was the loveliest, proudest-born and most alive figure John had seen in a long time. It annoyed hm to feel compromised by this situation.

'So you are Catherine Stratton—Thomas's wife.'

'I am Catherine Stratton. I trust you and your steward have come alone—that there isn't a troop of Parliament soldiers encamped outside the castle walls?'

'Be assured there is not—just a small escort of four men who are being attended to by your guards. Although my cousin's—your husband's—adherence to King Charles has been noted.'

'I imagine it has. Hopefully Cromwell's soldiers will keep away.'

'If they don't, they will have no difficulty gaining entrance—your watchmen weren't at their posts.'

'Do I detect criticism in your remark, sir?' she said coldly. 'It is my hope along with every person in England that the wars are over and the defence of one's property can be relaxed.'

'I beg your pardon. My words were not meant as a criticism, Lady Stratton, merely of concern. Since the fighting stopped the country is full of displaced men roaming freely and taking what can be had from lone travellers and properties with a relaxed guard. One cannot be too careful even now. I apologise if my presence offends you. Knowing your husband was a Royalist, I assume you, as his wife, must be also.'

Her lips curled in a wry smile. 'You assume too readily, sir. Just because my husband was a Royalist does not make me one.'

'Were you not of one mind?'

'No man makes up my mind for me,' she assured him, leaving him to decide which side she favoured. 'But I will tell you this. If it would cause the wind to blow fair for England, I might well turn my mind and heart to either side. Of late it has blown noticeably colder.'

'It is not the wind that grows cold, Lady Stratton. Say rather that it is the times in which we live that cause one to feel an inner and outer chill.'

'You may say what you please about the weather, but it is colder still in the prisons in which those loyal to the King are incarcerated.'

'It is common for wives to follow their husband's beliefs,' John said, watching her through narrowed eyes. It was difficult to read her. Unless he was mistaken, he sensed she could see no other point than her own. Perhaps the years of living at Carlton Bray Castle in an area strong in its support for King Charles had taken a firm hold of her, John thought, deeply troubled. May God help her if indeed this was the case.

'So, you have brought Thomas's body home,' Lady Stratton said. 'Well, you are now the new owner of Carlton Bray. Do you intend to take up residence immediately?' Her voice, clipped and businesslike, cut across the distance between them.

John did not reply at once. There was something solitary and untouchable about her. He could feel the young woman's nerves stretched taut as a bowstring, perhaps at that limit of tension that comes before it snapped, which he thought might have been brought about by his arrival. 'Not immediately—no. I am in no hurry. I am to meet with Thomas's lawyers eventually. Unfortunately they are in London so it will have to wait. As Thomas's wife and a beneficiary, it is necessary that you hear what they have to say. I have not been to Carlton Bray since I was a youth. I am curious to see if it is as I remember before riding on to London.'

'The funeral will take place immediately. I have notified Reverend Armstrong and everything is in readiness.'

John nodded. 'Then tomorrow would suit us all. I am also here at the bequest of your father.'

She did not answer at once. A slight narrowing of her eyes was her only reaction. What went on behind the cool visage John could only guess at.

'I see. Why did he not come himself?'

'He—is busy.'

She gave him a wry look, her eyes never leaving his face. 'My father has always been too busy to waste his time with his family. He is not concerned with what I do. Are you closely linked to my father?'

'I am. We know each other from our dealings during the war and our mutual relationship to Thomas. He and my father were friends of long standing.'

'Yes—I recall the Stratton name being talked about when I was a child, but I was young and paid little attention.'

'You father sends tidings and his apologies for not coming himself. He has written you a letter.' He produced a letter from inside his doublet.

'Then I suppose I should be thankful for small mercies. How considerate of him to write to his daughter at last,' she said in an acerbic tone. 'I wonder what he wants.'

'Have you not thought that he might want to see you—for yourself?'

A faint, contemptuous smile touched her lips. 'If that is so and he wishes to make amends for his neglect of me, then it is too little and too late.' Descending the two remaining steps, she walked towards him, holding out her hand. Taking the letter, she read the words carefully. When she had finished reading she strode to the fire and tossed it into the flames and watched it burn.

John was struck by her proud, easy carriage as she walked. She was stately and immensely dignified.

'It is as I thought,' she said. 'Having heard of Thomas's death, he writes that it is his wish that I go to him at Oakdene House—though God knows why. I want none of it—of him.'

'You are hard on your father. Clearly you do not see eye to eye.'

She was silent, considering his words, then she turned, her eyes capturing his. 'No. We have never got on. Would that I could. It is his fanatical obsession with this infernal war that I hate.'

'He works for the good of the realm.'

Her lips curled wryly. 'My father works for the good of himself, Edward Kingsley, and no one else. He was for the King before the King raised his standard at Nottingham. Deciding that England would be better and more comfortable under Parliament rule he became a turncoat, whose politics are as variable as the seasons. If you know him at all well, sir, you will know I speak the truth. He is his own worst enemy and is apt to be pulled in different ways than most ordinary mortals. I, too, want what is best for the realm, but my idea of bringing this about is different from that of my father.'

John paused to master himself and marshal his arguments. Catherine Stratton's views, whose animosity to Edward Kingsley's opinions as seen from a daughter's perspective, were of a different nature to his own. 'I imagine they are and am most interested for you to enlighten me.'

'Do not mock me, sir. I am not my father. He loves the power he wields over others. He wants control, believing he is the strong one. He does not hold women in very high regard—especially me—and his wife, my stepmother, only a little higher than me. Blanche was much younger than him when he married her. He wanted a son—was desperate for an heir to inherit his estate. He had no interest in daughters—in me. It must have been a disappointment to him when I was born. There were two children born to my mother after me—she miscarried them both. My father used me as a pawn in the marriage stakes, marrying me to your cousin because he was a good prospect without consulting me.'

'Yet your loyalty to your father in doing his bidding was commendable.'

She withstood his hard stare. 'I was just sixteen years old. Loyalty weighs nothing against reality. The haste with which my father married me to Thomas was embarrassing—although not without its advantages for both of them. It was a union to bring power and wealth to both families. Assured that Thomas would follow his lead, he was disappointed when he declared for the King, steadfast in his loyalty. I have no doubt that now he has discovered that Thomas is dead, he has found someone else for me to marry. Although why he thinks I would I want to wed again is beyond me. I can think of no man I would want to marry. Female I might be, but do not underestimate me. I own no man my superior.'

'The devil you do!' He was astonished. 'You have an uncommon honesty about such matters—unlike most women.'

There was a gleam of battle in her eyes as she held his gaze. 'There are many men hereabouts who see my independence as a threat. I prefer my own authority over what is mine.'

'Without having to answer to a husband. It appears to me that Thomas's death has come as something of a convenience to you. Did you not miss him?'

Her eyes hit sharply on his. 'You are impertinent, sir, but since you ask—no, I did not. We did not get on and I will not pretend otherwise. My father arranged my marriage to Thomas as a means to an end. And you, sir? Do you have a wife?'

'No. Life's too short to be bound to one woman.'

The war years had exacted a huge toll not only on the country, but on John's family also—he had lost both his father and older brother in the struggle. Holding a cynical view of love and marriage, he was reluctant to commit himself to any one woman.

'But you need an heir—all men need an heir, do they not? It is a priority.'

'Not in my case. I have brothers enough who have sons. When I propose marriage to the woman I want to spend the rest of my life with, it will not be for the purpose of begetting an heir. I take it you will not consider marrying a man of your father's choosing in the future.'

'No, I will not. I am my own woman, sir, and now I know that Thomas is indeed dead, then I will not be swayed from going my own way by any words of persuasion from my father. I will be much happier to remain a widow for the rest of my life. I have not seen Thomas for four years—four years of not knowing if I am wife or widow. Not even a letter. Now I know what has happened to him it feels as if a huge burden has been lifted from my shoulders.'

John detected the underlying bitterness in her words. He'd already determined her marriage to Thomas had not been a happy affair and that he had not dealt well with her. How much pain and anguish did this woman hide behind that calm composure? he wondered. He'd come to Carlton Bray expecting to find a quiet young woman grieving for her husband. Instead of this he'd found a strong, opinionated woman who appeared to be relieved he was dead.

'You are both forthright and honest, my lady. I admire your plain, frank candour. After all my experience with dissemblers I have come across, it is refreshing to hear plain speaking. That I cannot fault.'

Her eyes narrowed with suspicion at his words of praise and then she laughed. 'You are chivalrous, sir. I respect that.'

Her sudden and unexpected laughter was both joyous and warm. John suspected it was a long time since she had laughed at all. He suffered a slight sense of shock as, still smiling, she looked at him fully. There was something in her eyes that set his heart beating uncomfortably fast. He felt a great sense of excitement, and he could not but marvel at himself. She was a stranger to him with a mind of her own. Yet somehow he knew that beneath Catherine Stratton's exterior there was a lush sensuality. Instinctively he knew, too, that no matter how arrogant she might conceivably be, she had that magic quality that could well enslave a man and bring him to his knees.

'I have ridden many miles, my lady, to bring Thomas back to where he belongs,' he said, giving no indication of his thoughts and feelings where she was concerned. 'I was in the north with your father at the time of my cousin's death. When we parted company, as Thomas's heir I rode south to view my inheritance. It was your father's intention to go to Oakdene. He has asked me to escort you to London—he threatened me with God knows how many disasters if I came without you. I am reluctant to return to him to admit my mission has failed.'

'You will have to—unless you were to consider using force.'

'Heaven forbid if I were to resort to that. I can imagine the trouble you would cause me on the journey were I to take you under duress. You might, of course, find me an objectionable escort.'

'Not in the least. I do not know you well enough for that.'

'Are you not afraid of me and what I might do should you refuse to abide by your father's wishes?'

She smiled thinly. 'You give yourself too much credit. I'm a survivor. I do not show fear or weakness. That isn't part of who I am. I don't normally fraternise with the enemy—because that is what you will become if you insist on doing my father's bidding.' Her words were cool and measured. Defiance and strength shone from her. Being the only offspring of Edward Kingsley meant there was small chance of her escaping the same. Her path had been set at birth.

'So is it your intention to remain here until…when?'

'Worry not, sir. I will not be here when you come to take up your inheritance. Although should that happen before the country's troubles have been laid to rest, there may be discord when you do. It will soon be the talk of the village that your political leanings are different to those of my husband and every man hereabouts.'

'True, we differ, but it is not insurmountable.'

'Still, it is hardly the situation for domestic harmony. Most of the people hereabouts are loyal to the King, but in recent months as they have watched Parliament take the upper hand, they are sensible enough to keep their mouths shut about it.'

'As you do, Lady Stratton.'

She smiled. 'I like to keep my thoughts to myself.'

'And should the strife continue? Forgive me, Lady Stratton, but a wayward band of desperate stragglers from either side looking for succour could prove dangerous.'

"I am not alone and, with the castle walls to defend me, I am certainly not vulnerable.'

John admired her confidence. She had the backbone to withstand the defence of Carlton Bray as many beleaguered wives had done whose husbands were away fighting on either side. 'Despite the fact that there is an absence of competent guards on the gates, as I have already stated.' He looked at the old servant and then back at her. 'Should Commonwealth troops arrive at your door when I have gone you will need to have men-at-arms aplenty to guard you. These are still dangerous times.'

'We have survived so far—although the war has left behind physical scars which I am sure you must have observed for yourself when you rode in. The last I heard, the Scots who were marching south were stopped at Preston by Cromwell and driven back. The Royalists have been routed, Lord Fitzroy, and scattered throughout the length and breadth of England—something which you are aware of and rejoice, I am sure.'

'Fully aware, since I was there, but I do not rejoice in another's defeat. Preston was the death blow to the Royalists. They surrendered to Lord Fairfax. Many were killed, many taken prisoner—some of the leaders were sentenced to death, Thomas included. Badly wounded, he escaped over the border into Scotland.'

'I see. That still doesn't explain where he has been since Marston Moor.'

'I don't know the facts, but what I do know is that he was always involving himself in further uprisings wherever they occurred.'

'Instead of coming home—or having the goodness to let me know where he was. A brief note would have sufficed. Love him or loathe him, sir, I was still his wife and deserved better than that.'

'Whatever you say about Thomas's character, it was not his intention to be cruel to you.'

She looked at him coldly. 'And you would know that, would you? Since I do not believe we have much to fear just now you can tell my father I am happy to remain where I am, until I decide to go my own way.'

'There is something I have not told you, which may alter your decision on whether to go with me to London or not.'

'Oh? And what is that, pray?'

'Your father is not a well man. He was taken ill when he was in the north. The physician is treating him for a weakness of his heart.'

She stared at him. Clearly this had come as something of a shock to her. 'Are you telling me that my father is dying, sir?'

'Perhaps not as bad as that, but his suffering was so severe that he had to be escorted home. He has expressed his desire to see you most strongly.'

She cast him a frowning glance. 'I see.'

'Do you still intend to remain here?' His gaze was steady and challenging. 'I would advise against it.'

Catherine raised her chin a notch, not ready to be bullied. 'I haven't made up my mind.'

'Then you should. There is another issue that needs your consideration. Oakdene is close to London. You need to be present when Thomas's will is read.'

They stood face to face while arrogance and self-will waged their own war between them.

'Yes, there is that—although there is nothing to stop him informing me of the contents by letter. Obviously, if my father is seriously ill, I shall have to give it some thought.' She snapped a peremptory signal to the servant. 'Bring some ale and cold meats for our guests, Miles.'

John noted that, as she instructed the servants, authority wrapped itself about her like a cloak and she wore it comfortably.

'Remove your wet clothes and make yourselves comfortable by the fire. Miles will attend to your needs. Now excuse me. I have things to do.' To put an end to the discussion, she crossed to the stairs.

'Lady Stratton.' She halted mid-stride and looked back at him. 'I trust you will consider your answer most seriously. I came here in good faith. Even if you do decide against going to London, at least I have told you the truth about your father.'

With a slight nod of her head she turned from him. 'I am obliged.'

John watched her go. She walked with a purposeful stride and a proud set of her head. How would she react, he wondered, if she knew the truth about her husband's death and knew what lay in store for her when she reached her father's house?

After issuing orders to the housekeeper and a young maid to assist Miles in attending to the comforts of Lord Fitzroy and his steward, Catherine took refuge in her chamber. Standing at the window, she looked out, but saw nothing. The splendid room seemed to melt away and she was so cold as if she had been miraculously transported out of doors into the cold rain that continued to fall. Her shoulders sagged and her hands hung heavy by her sides. Her father was ill. How ill? she wondered. She suspected it had to be of a serious nature for him to summon her. Every instinct within her screamed resistance, but deep in her heart she knew she would have to go to him. Her heart was full, too full to express what had taken root deep within her. It was as unexpected as it was unwelcome. It was a tolling bell, heralding doom.

When she had married Thomas she had been a normal, healthy girl, filled with dreams and wishes about marriage, having read her share of romantic tales. Marriage to her was about mutual love, understanding and trust. She soon had reason to condemn herself for the silly, childish illusion, for marriage to Thomas was nothing like that. At the time, she had raised no objection to the marriage as she imagined it as a way to escape her father's domination of her, to be released from the hold he'd had on her since the death of her mother.

How wrong she had been. Thomas had never been a popular member of the community. Of an aggressive nature and downright unpleasant, he had left her alone to while away her days as she wished. He had found her so unattractive that he seldom came to her bed, fumbling clumsily and hurting her with his gropings when he did. In the beginning she had blamed herself for being naive and inexperienced so the fault had to lie with her. But when she listened to the girls she employed in the castle laughing and giggling to each other about their amorous encounters with the opposite sex, she knew there had to be more to what happened between a man and a woman when they were in bed.

She often wondered if Thomas found his pleasures elsewhere, but finding it both hurtful and distasteful to imagine that he might, she immediately banished the thought from her mind. There were times when she was lonely without another woman to talk to, or anyone to keep her company at night when the chill of winter permeated every inch of the castle.

She did not grieve her husband's loss, only what his loss would mean to her personally, to her future. This shamed her, but that was how it was. Mercilessly, she was to be thrust once more into her father's hands. There was a time, when she was a child and her mother had been alive, that he had shown her affection. Life had been so much more light-hearted then, when she had indulged in innocent pleasures. How she had longed for him to comfort her in her loss when her mother died, to show her that he still cared. But he was a man not given to exposing his feelings or emotions and now he was demanding that she go to London.

The brief, cherished dream of going to Wilsden Manor, a beautiful property in Hereford left to her by her mother, of living for herself and doing with her life exactly what she liked, was melting away just when it was almost within her grasp. After she had been to Oakdene she would go there, but at this time she was duty-bound to abide by her father's wishes. Was it foolish of her to hope that the long-held memories of the affection he had shown her in childhood could be revived?

Her thoughts shifted to John Stratton. Unlike Thomas, who was tall and thickset, with unattractive square features and fair hair thinning at the crown, John Stratton was quite different. But she must never forget that he was a Stratton, that he was of the same blood as Thomas, and her initial impression was that he was as arrogant and demanding as Thomas has been. At thirty-one years old, he was a striking-looking man with an enormous presence. Although his manners were perfectly correct, she sensed in him a purposefulness that made her uneasy. He was of an impressive stature, tall and lean and as straight as an arrow, with a whipcord strength that promised toughness, and, even though his arrival had interrupted the peaceful running of the castle, she could not help but admire the fine figure he made.

His dark brown hair sprang thickly, vibrantly from his head and curled about his neck. His chin was jutting and arrogant, his mouth firm, hinting at stubbornness that could, she thought, prove dangerous, making him a difficult opponent if pushed too far. There was also a hardness about him, an inflexibility of mind and will, and a toughness imbued by his military life.

Yet there were laughter lines at the corners of his mouth that bespoke humour. But it was his eyes that had held her. They were compelling, brilliant blue and vibrant in the midst of so much uncompromising darkness and, when they had settled on her, they had been unnervingly intent. He had seemed to take pleasure in studying every inch of her, although there was no lechery in his gaze.

Somehow she could sense he expected her to fear him and to fidget nervously under his regard. It was for this very reason that she had stood motionless, forcing herself to look directly back at him, giving him stare for stare. And then he had smiled, a thin, crooked smile revealing a lightning glimpse of very white teeth. His masculinity was obvious and complete and there was a certain refinement in his well-defined, handsome features. All through their meeting she had been uncomfortably conscious of him and was careful not to move too close. She would not be lulled by a handsome face.

What did he make of her? And did he wonder about her loyalties—King or Parliament? It didn't worry her that he might regard her as having the same faults and allegiances as Thomas—and, she thought on a sigh, there were times when she had to question them herself.

The morning of Thomas Stratton's funeral dawned dank and grey. After a night with little sleep, Catherine woke early. She rose and crossed to the window to look out. The rain had ceased and a grey mist swathed the top of the hills and drifted down into the valley bottoms. As she looked down into the courtyard a form, probably one of the grooms, moved towards the stables. Suddenly, a ride out into the surrounding hills before breakfast was too tempting for her to resist. She often rode out early morning and, she thought, this could well be the last time she would do so at Carlton Bray.

Pulling on her clothes and riding boots and carrying her hat, she silently slipped down the stairs and left the castle. As she'd crossed the hall, she imagined she heard the sound of a horse's hooves clattering over the drawbridge, but on entering the yard and seeing no one, she thought she had been mistaken. The stables were quiet, the horses shifting restlessly in their stalls. Hurriedly saddling her mount, she breathed deeply of the scent of hay and the warm bodies of the horses which she always found familiar and comforting.

Leaving the castle behind, she rode towards the hills. The paths were familiar to her and she rode her horse hard, revelling in the exercise. Yet she had a heavy heart, for this might be the last time she rode these hills which were so much a part of her life. When her beloved mother had died and since marrying Thomas, followed by his rejection of her and long absence, she had at first floundered in uncertainty with no confidante, no one to hear her complaints and give her succour. Carlton Bray had become the centre of her existence, her beating heart. When she realised that this was her life from now on, she had moved in a carefully constructed calm efficiency, directing the household and supervising what had to be done in times of strife, of which there were many. She had come to love every ancient and battle-pitted stone of the old castle and would miss it terribly, but life had to go on.

After half an hour and having ridden some distance from the castle, she toyed with the notion of turning back, then dismissed the idea. Thomas's funeral loomed like a dark cloud over the day ahead of her and she wanted to enjoy her ride a bit longer. Taking a path that would lead her up into the hills, she decided to ride as far as the lake, which was a thin ribbon of water in a thickly wooded valley. Taking a downward path, which was thickly choked with briars, deftly her horse picked its way along. Catherine knew that when she broke through the trees the view would be well worth it. She was not mistaken. It was a view she had seen many times and revelled in its beauty in all the changing seasons.

Abruptly the foliage parted. From where she stopped a stretch of clear ground cut a swathe some twelve feet in width. To her left, further along the lake, large rocks protruded out of deep water. Dismounting, she took the reins and quietly made her way along the edge of the trees, her gaze fixed on the rocks ahead of her, certain she had heard the soft whicker of a horse. About to step around the rocks forming a sequestered cove screened by a tangle of willows, she quickly stepped back, having seen a horse nibbling the grass and a pile of clothes on the rocks. Moments later there was a splash, followed by the lesser sound and sight of a body, like a dark, sleek blade, cutting its way just below the surface of the water with slow, controlled strokes.

Catherine took a wary step out of the covering willow tree to watch as the swimmer ploughed his way into the centre of the lake, his strokes powerful and sure. She shuddered, thinking that whoever it was would surely freeze to death in the cold November waters of the lake. A thin mist floated just above the surface. She drew back when he turned and swam back to the rocks, then rose ghostlike from the water. His dark hair hung in wet strands about his head and neck. Without even seeing his face Catherine knew he was John Stratton. The water level dropped from his chest to his waist, to his thighs and—she wanted to turn and run, but did not, held in place by the sight of the primeval, glistening form, naked and powerful.

Spellbound, Catherine let her gaze rove over the firm muscled chest and legs, lingering on the patch of dark hair and his manhood protruding there. Despite the coldness of the morning her body became heated, her face red, yet she could not tear her eyes away. Unaware that he was being watched, he began to dress.

Rooted to the spot. Catherine continued to watch, her breath ragged and her heart beating loud in her ears. She was careful not to make a sound lest he heard, having no idea how she would explain her presence. How she managed to keep herself hidden until he'd mounted his horse and ridden off she couldn't say, but she was relieved when the sound of his horse's hooves could no longer by heard.

Only then did she leave the lake and ride back to Carlton Bray. When she rode into the courtyard she didn't see the figure standing watching her, no more than a silhouette in the shadows—tall, physically imposing, arrogant even, a ghost of a smile playing on his lips.

Chapter Two

The small community of Carlton village made the effort to attend Lord Stratton's funeral to pay their respects. Along with a few gentlemen and their wives from neighbouring manors and tenant farmers from surrounding farms, they made their solemn progress through the heavy doors of the small Saxon church—although more had come to take a look at the new lord than to remember the old. When the widow of Lord Stratton entered in heavy black mourning, along with Lord Thomas's heir, the congregation nodded their collective heads in solemn respect. Lady Stratton had never put on airs, but her breeding was written all over her. She was every inch a lady, in her speech, in her manners, in the way she moved, no matter what she wore, be it plain gowns or breeches.

Lord Fitzroy and Lady Stratton took their seats in the ornately carved pew kept for the Stratton family—although there had been few of late to fill it. The members of the household sat behind them. Many knew of the new landowner and owner of Carlton Bray Castle, that he was Earl Fitzroy of the Sussex branch of the Stratton family and a staunch Parliamentarian who would, without doubt, have great influence in county politics.

Reverend Armstrong, in a suit of black with an austere collar as white as his shock of hair, read from the new prayer book approved by Parliament from the lectern. There were no words spoken in Latin, no vestments, ornate candlesticks or candles now Parliament ruled. The prayers were long, as was the eulogy, outlining the life and deeds of Thomas Stratton in the cold church.

Catherine's face was grim as the service went on around her, her mouth pressed in a hard line as she looked straight ahead, giving no indication of her thoughts or emotions. She had been brought up in a house that had taught her it was not done to show one's feelings in public, not even grief for the death of a loved one—not that she had loved Thomas and had little respect for the man who had virtually ignored her for all of their married life.

From the pulpit, the minister eloquently launched into the many attributes of her husband, of which she heard not a word. She bent her head and uttered the words of the prayers, conscious of the man beside her, his head bent in prayer.

The memory of what she had seen on her early morning ride she found impossible to banish from her mind, or the image of how he had looked when he had risen from the waters of the lake. Her nipples hardened beneath the fabric of her clothes as the picture of him standing there, legs partially spread, hands on hips as he stared straight ahead made her body tremble. She tried to imagine how it might have been if she had stepped out of the undergrowth and stripped off her clothes—how his eyes would flash with lust and stare at her unconcealed breasts. Her mind travelled down the imaginary path his hands would take, touching lightly here and there, with fingers inscribing small circles around the taut, distended nipples before brushing lightly over her aching thighs.

Suddenly the minister's voice intruded, scattering her impious thoughts, but they hovered and played on the perimeter of her mind and a little rebellious smile curved her lips. As if sensing a change in her, her companion glanced at her. Their gazes held for a moment in quiet perusal and then she lowered her head as a knowing flush mantled her cheeks and she forced herself to behave as a recently widowed woman should.

Then it was over and they watched as Thomas's earthly remains were interred with his ancestors in the Stratton family vault that a forebear had built close to the altar in the church. It was neither vanity nor morbidity, just confidence that life would be followed by death and the Manor would continue in the hands of the Strattons of the Sussex line. Lord Fitzroy left the pew and stood aside for Catherine to pass. From the moment they had come together to journey to the church in the coach, he was nothing but courtesy itself. He was thoughtful and charming, and Catherine displayed an attitude that told him she was grateful and glad of his support.

The congregation rose and filed out. Passing through into the churchyard, Catherine saw that the sun was out in a sky streaked with the last remnants of cloud. It gave her no pleasure. It seemed that it had come out to mock her, for she knew she had no power, no weaponry, against her father's hold on her. The future no longer seemed appealing or safe. Now everything was changed and she was no longer sure of anything. She was adrift.

John kept to her side as she graciously accepted the condolences of those who came to pay their respects, some clearly moved that she was leaving Carlton Bray after so many years.

Standing apart from the rest, a woman with two young children clinging to her skirts drew her attention. A smile appeared on Catherine's face and she went to have a word with her, John standing within hearing.

'Mrs Jenkins! It's good to see you. How are things at home? Better, I hope.'

'Yes, thank you, my lady. I wanted to come and bid you farewell and to thank you for what you did for me and the children.'

'Not at all. I was glad to help. How is young Jimmy?'

'Better. The doctor assures me there will be no lasting effects.'

'That's good to hear. And your husband?'

'Home at last, thank the Lord.'

Mrs Jenkins moved off when others came to speak to Lady Stratton.

After thanking Reverend Armitage for the service, they climbed into the coach that was to take them back to the castle, where a light repast had been prepared for the guests.

'That woman—Mrs Jenkins,' Lord Fitzroy said. 'She lives in the village?'

'No—half a mile away. She has four children. Her eldest, Jimmy, was picked on by some boys in the village because of his father's loyalty to Cromwell. He was beaten quite badly—thank goodness he will make a full recovery. His mother was afraid and vulnerable so, along with her children, I brought her into the castle until the hostility against the family died down.'

'That was noble of you.'

'Noble? No. I was doing my Christian duty. That was the way I saw it. Her husband has returned from the war so now she has someone to protect her.'

'And I have no doubt she will be eternally grateful to you. You are well-liked and respected in these parts. I could see that. I imagine you will be greatly missed.'

'Yes,' she replied softly, averting her eyes. 'I will miss them, also. We have shared some difficult times. I pray for a brighter future for them all.'

Seated across from her companion, her face pale and unable to conceal the tension inside her, she sensed that he must be contemplating the immensity Thomas's passing would inflict on her, aware that she had already suffered so much. But she was strong and resilient and one thing she would not do was allow her will and her strength to desert her.

'The funeral is over,' he said, as if reading her thoughts. 'Take as long as you think is necessary to come to terms with what has happened. You are tired and hurting and it will take time.'

Catherine stared at him. Never had a man's nearness, the sound of his voice, been so welcome. She saw compassion in his eyes. His gaze was heavy, giving her sympathy, assuring her without words of protection. She felt lost, as if all feeling had frozen inside her. Never had she felt so alone and she did not like it. She had nothing to sustain her, nothing from her marriage to Thomas but misery and toil, no happy memories. Tears would not avail her, as she knew now, beyond the mercy of a doubt, for this one terrible hurt, this loneliness, there was no cure at all.

'This is my worst nightmare come true,' she said, feeling that the excruciating day's events seemed to have eaten into the deepest crannies of her mind. 'There is nothing left for me here—and God knows I have tried. And now my father has summoned me back to London—to Oakdene. Why should I go there now? There is nothing for me there, either. I seem to have been drifting aimlessly in the shadows for so long that I've forgotten there's another world beyond Carlton Bray.'

'Whether you want to go to your father or not is

beside the point. Think about it. He was very ill when we parted at Newcastle, the journey south will have weakened him further. If he should die, you will never forgive yourself for not going to him. Listen to him, to what he has to say, while showing him that you are capable of running your own life.'

'It is easy for you to say that,' she retorted, her anxieties written in deep lines on her face. 'You don't understand. How can you? I imagine you have a loving family waiting for you. I have no one. I must reconcile myself to a life of desolation and learn to fend for myself.' She thought she saw a darkening to his eyes when she mentioned his family, but it was soon gone and she dismissed it from her mind.

'All the more reason for you to come with me when I leave here. Do not pity yourself. You are above that. The way I see it you have no alternative. When today is over you must prepare to leave.'

'Must?' she uttered sharply. 'There is nothing I *must* do.'

'This time you will,' he said coldly.

She looked at him uncomprehendingly. His strong, handsome face had become stern and uncompromising. She was beginning to know that look. Its power was not to be underestimated. He was angry with her and his words brought a pain to her heart that was sharper than a blade. But she kept it at bay—there would be time to feel later. Her own ire under his bright blue stare diminished and, lowering her eyes, she continued on a calmer note.

'I told you I would think about it and I will. Just how well do you know my father?'

'We have seen much of each other since the war began, at one battle or another—we even fought side by side on occasion. At Edgehill, back in forty-two, he was wounded and knocked from his horse. He truly believed it was the end. I saw what happened and, despite suffering a minor wound myself, we managed to get off the field together. I got to know him well. He is a man with a deep sense of integrity and courage. Fighting in battle hurts a man's mind as well as his body. Tragedy touches all of us. Your father gave me his support when I was going through a difficult time.'

'And you were hurting?'

'I was, but I didn't realise how much. Your father helped me deal with that. I knew what I had to do, but it was hard for me to take another human life. I couldn't stomach it.'

'But you had to do it.'

He nodded. 'Our time in the war was hard, but our special relationship made us close. I suppose you could say that he saved me from myself. I have been a guest at Oakdene House many times when I've been in London. You have already told me that the two of you are at odds with each other.'

'Yes—and for many reasons. I do not know the man you speak of. You have seen a side to him that is unknown to me. My mother was not cold in the ground before he found himself another wife—Blanche, the beautiful and ambitious daughter of Lord Aniston of Murton House in York.'

'We do not choose our families. My own…' He paused, seeming to recollect himself. 'It might help you to realise that, to some degree or other, we all have difficult families.'

His words had Catherine wondering what he could mean, but he said no more and she did not ask. But she was curious.

'And—do you not see eye to eye with Blanche either?' he enquired.

'Far from it, but I have learned to cope with my stepmother in my own way, which is largely to avoid her whenever possible. That isn't difficult with half the country between us. I thought this would be simple when I married Thomas and being so far away from London, but they made a point of coming here before Thomas went off to fight the King's cause. Father hoped he would change his allegiance and failed.'

'Was that the last time you saw your father?'

'Yes—almost six years ago. Blanche is a schemer, a woman who knows what she wants and does everything within her power to get it—although I do not think it was of any help when her parents married her to my father, though I believe they were happy for a time.' She noted how John was looking at her, his brow furrowed in a thoughtful frown. He must wonder at the underlying bitterness she had expressed earlier when she had spoken of Thomas. He was probably surprised that she would speak of something so personal, so intimate. Her sudden burst of anger had brought a flush to her cheeks.

'Please don't upset yourself. It doesn't matter now.'

'It does matter,' she uttered forcefully. She could not help herself. She had never spoken out against her stepmother, but years of bottling it up inside her had festered and become something she must rid herself of. 'It matters to me. She never had a kind word for me or spoke up for me when I raised my objections to marrying Thomas. Indeed, despite being married to my father, I believe she had an eye for Thomas herself—and he was not averse to her either, I regret to say.' She caught John's eyes speculatively. 'You have met Blanche. You must know what she is like.'

He looked away. 'We have met on several occasions, when I have been a guest in your father's house, but I have not been in her company for any length of time.' His words gave nothing away, but Catherine heard an edge to his voice. His meetings with Blanche in the past had caused that cynical note, she was sure.

'Then consider yourself fortunate. One thing I learned from my mother at an early age was how to employ tact when it was most needed. With Blanche it was difficult, although I always tried hard not to let her upset me whenever I found myself in her company.'

John grinned and one dark brow arched and his eyes danced with devilish humour. 'If she offends you the next time you meet, perhaps you should call her out for the requisite twenty paces,' he said, gently teasing.

Catherine's lips answered the laughter in his eyes

in a broad smile which progressed into laughter of her own that revealed shining teeth. 'If I do, will you be my second, sir?'

John shook his head with mock gravity. 'I'm afraid that would not be appropriate. As a friend of your father it would be only right that I remain neutral. Besides, I think you are more than capable of taking care of yourself—and there is nothing that pleases a woman more than victory over another.'

'Oh? Please explain to me what you mean.'

'That when one woman strikes at the heart of another, she usually hits the target.'

Catherine's mouth twitched. 'You mean if I strike at my stepmother's heart, it could prove fatal?'

John's eyes danced as though he found their conversation about her stepmother vastly entertaining. 'It's possible—but in your stepmother's case I hope, for your own and your father's sake, it is an exception.' His expression became serious as he continued to hold her gaze. 'You should laugh more often,' he murmured. 'It suits you. Tell me, are you always so outspoken?'

'It's an attitude I seem to have grown into. No doubt you must have found some of my remarks quite outrageous and think that I'm dreadfully ill bred.'

'Nothing is further from my thoughts and, with Edward as your father, there is nothing ill-bred about you.'

'Be that as it may, but I think Thomas looked on the war as a godsend—to be relieved of me. I was soon an abandoned wife with a castle to take care of. It was as much as I could do to hold everything on the estate together and provide for those at the castle and the tenants. The fines, which I knew would come, would be crippling. Should Thomas have come back looking for funds, there would be nothing to spare to go in the King's coffers. Creditors are always at the door. If the bills are not paid soon, not only do we have the threat of sequestration hanging over us, but the bailiffs will come and carry everything away.'

'Don't fret. It is no longer your concern. It will be taken care of.'

As John uttered those words, he could not know what a relief that was to Catherine to have the burden of Castle Bray lifted from her shoulders.

They fell silent as the coach rattled over the drawbridge, much to Catherine's relief. Her companion's presence in the confines of the coach was beginning to scatter her senses and draw her attention to things she didn't want to notice. He directed her eyes like a sail blown by the wind. Before she knew it she would be wondering what it would be like to be kissed by him.

She sighed, directing her thoughts away from him, not looking forward to entertaining their more privileged neighbours. Not one of them had approached her during times of need. It was ironic that they should come today as though the past four years had never happened, to partake of the late Lord Stratton's liquor and to talk and rekindle old memories and dwell of the times they had shared that meant nothing to her.

* * *

When John climbed the battlements later it was to find a single figure standing alone, gazing at the village in the distance. There was a quiet, strangely frozen quality about her, as though her inner self weren't really there. Apart from a few bobbing lights, the village was in darkness. Everything was still and quiet. The rain had kept away and there was a cold sharpness to the night air. Built in the borderlands, wedged between the Welsh mountains and English river beds, the castle stood isolated in this sparsely populated slice of land. It was a lovely part of England—mountains and moorland, villages and castles, but also an area of frequent conflict.

The moon was bright and clear, and he saw that she was attired in her breeches. She was so still, perfect, exquisite, and she reminded him of a young warrior queen, proud and unyielding, her gaze owning all she surveyed, her profile sharp and clear, etched against the night sky. He had never met a woman like her. Her features were delicate and exquisitely lovely with none of the pampered softness of so many women he had known. She was earthy, sensual and complex and he admired everything about her. Since coming to Carlton Bray his thoughts had turned constantly to her. He thought he had never seen anything so beautiful. Slowly he moved towards her. She did not turn, but he sensed she knew when he stopped behind her. There was something strikingly lovely and dignified about her slender form.

'Why don't you come inside and warm yourself?' he said softly. 'It's a cold night.'

'Is it? I don't feel it.' There was a moment of silence between them before she continued. 'I hope your accommodation is suitable and that you have everything you require. When the mourners left I instructed the servants to have hot water carried to your quarters and to ensure the men accompanying you are well taken of.'

'Thank you. Everything is in order. Have you given any more thought to going to London?'

'Yes. You were right to persuade me. My father is ill. It would seem he leaves me with no choice. When do you wish to leave?'

'A couple of days, no more. Just long enough for you to put things in order here.'

'Thank you—although there is very little for me to do. When I heard that Thomas was dead I made preparations to leave.'

'I assume you have a steward to take care of things.'

'No. I do all that. All my time as been taken up with estate matters and living off rents I can collect—from those who can afford to pay, that is. Thomas found time to contribute most generously to the King's coffers before he left, leaving us in dire straits. Most of the men in the village and the surrounding area went to fight for the King. Some have returned and others—well— either dead or prisoners of Parliament. My steward and most of the servants went, leaving me with no one to help with the burden of running Carlton Bray.'

'I see. That must have been difficult.'

'It was.'

'Does your father know how you have struggled over the years?'

'No, I don't believe so. His mind was always occupied with events of the day and the politics of England. I always thought his views were too extreme. He holds an independent view on religion, favouring the new way of worship. He feared that Charles Stuart was being encouraged by his French wife to impose the Catholic rituals on his subjects. He sees the devil in theatricals and any form of frivolous entertainment and is opposed to any form of debauchery and frequently complains of overindulgence and extravagance, of which he accused the King's court of being rife.'

There would be little wonder if Blanche had favoured Thomas, John thought, who, despite taking the side of Parliament in the wars, believed in freedom in every sense. 'You don't have to worry about it any more. I will take care of everything. I shall leave Will Price. He and I have been together throughout the wars. He is a good man, capable and reliable. He has no family to go home to. I am sure he will have no objection to remaining here and taking charge of things in my absence. In fact, having listened to his desire—and more than a few complaints these past weeks, I might add—about finding a hearth on which to rest his weary feet, I have not the slightest doubt that he will welcome the suggestion to remain here.'

Catherine seemed surprised by what he was offering. 'He would do that?'

'I am sure of it. I'll discuss the matter with him later.'

'That would be most welcome. Miles, who has lived at Carlton Bray for many years, will give him the benefit of his knowledge concerning the estate. Indeed, I think he knows more about the running of the estate than Thomas ever did.'

'I gather from what you have told me that yours was not a happy marriage, for which I am deeply sorry.'

Catherine turned her head and looked at him. 'I do not mean to speak ill of the dead, but Thomas was not a sensitive and caring husband. So, no, it wasn't a happy marriage.'

John felt a surge of anger. Her father should never have considered her marriage to Thomas, let alone allowed it. 'That must have been difficult for you.'

'Yes, it was. But enough of Thomas,' she said, seeming to relax a little and perching on the edge of the crenelated battlement. 'We hear so little of what is going on in the country, so tell me—what news is there of the King?'

'From what I understand he is a prisoner in Carisbrooke Castle on the Isle of Wight—although I believe he is given a certain amount of freedom since he has given his word of honour not to try to escape. A Parliamentary delegation has gone over there with notions of a compromise—the results of which we can only wait and see.'

'And if he does not comply? Can he be set aside? Can Parliament rule without him?'

John fell silent, watching her. After a moment, he said, 'If need be.'

'And Henrietta Maria, the Queen?'

'She is in France, trying to raise money for her husband's cause'

'Then his cause is hopeless. What will be done with him?'

'If they take him back to London, they will make him swear never again to raise an army to be used against the people of England or elsewhere for that matter. He will also have to learn to work with Parliament, not against it and with bishops. In other words, he will have to rule on the permission of Parliament, on Parliament's terms.'

'I cannot imagine him agreeing to do that.'

'No, neither can I.'

'Whatever happens in the future, he believed he was right in doing what he did. That has to be taken into account when assessing people.'

'You are fair minded.'

'It is necessary for a king.'

'But he destroyed a nation when he took the country to war because he believed in his own right. I find it hard to forgive.'

'I agree. But the point is that he thought he was doing the best for his people.' Catherine got to her feet and looked out over the darkened land once more. 'The world has changed. Nothing will be the same again.'

He gazed down at her. 'Then let us pray the changes will be for the better. But one must never forget the conflicts in which so many lives were lost—on both sides. Good, honest Englishmen, fighting for what they believed to be right—be it for Parliament or the King. We must never forget that.'

'No, we must not,' Catherine replied, with a stirring of respect. 'Were you ever at the court of King Charles?'

'Yes, a long time ago, before the wars when neighbour was set against neighbour and people had to choose which side to support—King or Parliament.'

'And is Henrietta Maria as beautiful as everyone says she is?'

John was amused as he studied her and couldn't help but smile a little. 'She is fair enough, I suppose, but each to his own. I only went there once. There were better things to do than idle away one's time at Court with its backbiting and gossip and scandals. It all appeared cordial on the surface, made up of civilised human beings, but there were many dangerous and treacherous undercurrents as ambitious courtiers solicited the King and Queen's favour and schemed to better their positions and fill their family coffers.'

'And were you not ambitious?'

'No,' he said decidedly. 'I was not influential in Court matters and never sought favour. I knew in which direction I was heading and it was not to take on the King's cause.' He smiled suddenly. 'Although I imagine you would have found it intriguing—the

Queen always admired an intellectual mind. But there was so much warmongering among the ladies who surrounded the Queen, with their petty jealousies and intrigues, weaving webs of deceit. And the gentlemen were equally as bad, with their love of corruption, of besting the next man in the frequent games they played. Would you have liked to have met the Queen?'

'I suppose I would. I heard she was much admired by the gentlemen of the Court.'

'She is the Queen—and a Frenchwoman. It flattered her vanity to be surrounded by men and she was not averse to a handsome face.'

Catherine shot him a little smile. 'And did you not aspire to be one of them?'

'No, I did not. But those days are gone. The Court of King Charles held no attraction for me and much less the Queen herself.'

'Without the Royal Court and living under the rule of Parliament made up of Puritans and the like, it will be hard to adjust to a world without the colour and flamboyance of the gentry and the aristocracy, of masquerades and balls and music. What a dull place England will become.' Catherine was silent for a moment, seeming preoccupied with her thoughts. 'I often come up here at night when I cannot sleep.'

'Are there many nights like that?'

'Too many.

'I'm sorry. You are unhappy.'

She shrugged. 'I am used to it. I like to look towards

the village, wondering what the people are doing and about their families.'

'I used to come up here often. In daylight, as I well remember, the view of the Welsh Marches is astounding and the panorama goes on for miles and miles.'

'So it does.'

'As boys, Thomas and I had great fun exploring the countryside hereabouts.'

She half turned her head towards him. 'Did you really? I can't imagine Thomas having fun. He was a dour character and always so serious. He was never at home—always fighting some battle somewhere. I think he preferred it that way.'

'You say you heard nothing from him after Marston Moor?'

'No. I made enquires, but they came to nothing. Whether he was dead or in some prison somewhere, I had no idea—until your letter came informing me of his death. Did you know your cousin well?'

He nodded. 'My parents brought me to Carlton Bray on many occasions and Thomas would visit us at Inglewood—my home in Sussex. It's close to the sea so we spent most of our youth swimming and climbing the cliffs. Like many families in England at the time war broke out, divided loyalties separated us.'

'That must have hurt you terribly.'

He nodded, remembering the pain caused by the split Thomas's allegiance to the King had caused in the family, culminating in Thomas's ignominious death in Newcastle almost two weeks ago. He would blame himself for ever for not being there to speak for his cousin, whose death had brought degradation on all Strattons. There was nothing honourable in the manner of his death, when he had been hanged by the neck for his treasonable actions—an end so violent that he had decided not to disclose the manner of it to Thomas's wife. By not doing so, right or wrong, so be it.

'It did,' he said in answer to her question, 'profoundly, but it did not make me think less of him.'

'And how do you feel about inheriting the estate? I know you have your own acres and properties in Sussex. Is it your intention to take up residence here?'

'In truth, I haven't given it much thought and it is not the life I had planned. Richard, my older brother, was to have inherited Carlton Bray if Thomas did not produce a son—had he not met his death at the point of a Royalist sword at Edgehill.'

'And your father?'

John turned his head away to look into the night. 'He was killed at Marston Moor.' He fell silent for a moment, at one with his thoughts of his father. 'With Parliament confiscating Royalist properties, which would have been the case with Carlton Bray if Thomas had returned, now it has come to me it will remain within the family. And you? Have you given more thought to a future without Thomas? I feel a sense of duty for your comfort.'

'Please don't. You are not responsible for me, my lord, and need not concern yourself over my future. I expect to have jointure as Thomas's widow from the estate, but I also brought resources to the marriage. I inherited Wilsden Manor from my mother in Hereford. It's a lovely old place where my grandmother was raised and then my mother. I will go there after I have seen my father. I shall be comfortable there.'

'Who resides there?'

'A family acquaintance—a spinster lady, Mrs Amelia Sheldon. She took up residence before my mother died. When I married Thomas and went to live at Carlton Bray, I saw no reason to ask her to leave. I haven't been able to visit as often as I would have liked, but she has looked after the property well. Thankfully it has escaped the ravages of the Civil War. Be assured that if I go to London to see my father I will take my leave of him as soon as may be.'

He nodded, watching her closely. The depth of this young woman's composure amazed him, as did the delicate softness in the expressionless young face that was looking up at his. He had seen enough of her to realise she had many pleasing attributes and was surprised to find that she stirred his baser instincts. 'There is no need for haste—although I imagine your father will insist on keeping you with him for a while.'

For one moment her eyes blazed, glinting gold in the green depths, before she turned her head away. 'I doubt that, although he can insist all he likes. My father cares not who he hurts, or how many, as long as he gains his own selfish will. I am a widow and no longer beholden to him. I did not seek marriage to Thomas. I did not want it. I make no secret of the fact. It turned out to be a travesty, a hollow pretence. In time I *will* go to Wilsden, with or without my father's blessing.

He smiled. 'Good. I see your mind is made up. To-morrow I intend to take a look at the estate. Will you accompany me? You are familiar with the tenants and the land. I would like to gain some understanding of Carlton Bray before I leave.'

'Yes, I would be glad to.'

'Thank you. Now, will you come inside?'

She shook her head. 'I'll stay here a while. You go. Goodnight.'

'Goodnight—and—Catherine?'

She lifted her head. 'Yes?'

'I may call you that?'

'Yes. I would like that.'

'My name is John.'

After excusing himself, John turned from her and walked away and wondered why fate should have brought them together at this time. He thought long and hard about what she had told him and he was caught somewhere between concern and tenderness. He remembered the deep bitterness in her tone when she told him of her desolate years since her marriage to Thomas—they were the kind of images that were familiar to him, images of his own rejection by a father who had favoured one son above the other. Never would he forget the despairing feeling of rejection that had once turned his own life into a living hell.

It was Catherine's father who had brought him to a better understanding of his life and encouraged him in his military duties. How confused, alone and threatened Catherine must have felt when Thomas had brought her to Carlton Bray and left her alone while he had gone off to war—but she was resilient and had survived better than most young women would have done.

He couldn't understand why he was drawn to his cousin's widow in a way he had never been to any other woman, but there was nothing he could do. Meeting her had had an effect on him. Her pale features and those incredible green eyes amid the mass of deep golden hair had drawn him like a magnet. Already he was looking forward to riding out with her on the morrow.

The following morning dawned fine, with a cold breeze that carried the scent of the hills and shredded clouds that scurried across the sky. Standing there in the cobble yard in front of the stables, Catherine could smell damp hay and horseflesh, old leather and manure, an earthy, though not unpleasant, odour. She was securing the girth on her horse when she saw John striding towards her, the folds of his long black cloak falling from his broad shoulders. The high riding boots he wore seemed to emphasise the muscular length of his legs. Catherine hardly noticed anything going on around her, her attention entirely focused on him.

As her thoughts raced, he looked at her and smiled. In that moment she noticed again the startling, intense blue of his eyes, and again she thought how extraordinarily attractive he was. Her heart suddenly leapt into her throat in a ridiculous, choking way and she chided herself for being so foolish. He was, after all, a stranger to her. He looked at her searchingly, his deep, dark gaze missing nothing. She noted the look of unconcealed appreciation on his face as he surveyed her breeches and doublet beneath her cloak.

'I see you are ready to ride out,' he said, taking his horse from the groom who had saddled it upon his instruction. 'It's a fine day to take stock of things. Where do you suggest we start?'

At the sound of his voice Catherine experienced a rush of feeling, a bittersweet joy in view of all that had occurred the previous day. Before he had come to Carlton Bray she had felt a loneliness deep inside, but his just being there sent a message of warmth. 'I thought we might ride by some of the farms and head up to the hills—if that's agreeable. You will be able to meet some of the tenants.'

His smile curled and his lips lifted slightly at one corner. 'That would be perfect,' he said, hoisting himself up into the saddle. 'Lead on. I am entirely in your hands.'

Catherine thought that although he hadn't meant it to sound provocative, she interpreted it that way, causing her cheeks to redden with embarrassment. As if he had read her thought, his smile deepened and, laughing softly, he kicked his horse into action.

They were soon on their way, clattering across the drawbridge and leaving the castle behind, riding at a brisk gallop across countryside Catherine knew so well. They rode west, to the high hills, stopping at farms and cottages along the way. She was unaware that her hair, fastened back in the nape of her neck and left to hang free down her spine, was a hundred different shades and dazzling lights. Her eyes were sparkling like emeralds, bright with energy, and her senses drank in the intoxication of it all as they rode through wooded river valleys and on to the moorland uplands.

Catherine appreciated having a companion to ride with. She found her eyes drawn to John constantly, noting the authority, the strength held in check as he handled his horse. So many conflicting emotions swirled inside her, fighting for ascendancy. When he had appeared on the battlements the previous night, she had enjoyed talking to him and he had occupied her thoughts afterwards for a long time. Now, as she stole glances at him along the way, he was more attractive than ever and the need to be even closer to him was more vivid than before. Watching him, she was entranced, hardly breathing, as the sun came out from behind a cloud and a shaft of silver light settled on him.

Sensing her gaze, he turned his head and regarded her curiously. She saw the deepening light in his eyes, the long, silken lashes, the thick, defined, black brows, and wanted to touch him as one touches the feathers on a bird's wing. Immediately she turned her head away, realising that, before he had come, there had been a vast emptiness in her life that she did not want to admit to, like a clock that has stopped ticking.

* * *

After they had been riding for a couple of hours, they stopped at a village inn to partake of a bite to eat. They were conspicuous as they entered the inn. At John's presence, heads turned and people flattened themselves against the wall to let him pass. The landlord knew Lady Stratton and word had got around that Lord Fitzroy had arrived to look over his inheritance. He made them welcome, bringing out bread and cheese and lashings of butter and light ale to wash it down.

They ate in companionable silence, watching as people came and went on their journeys.

'I suspect you're going to miss all this,' John remarked, having eaten his fill and relaxing back on the settle and drinking his ale.

'Yes. I love it up here in the hills. I'll remember it always.' She looked across at him. 'As you have seen, there is much to do on the estate. I know you have your own properties in Sussex and I struggle to think how you will work this estate, there being a great distance between them.'

'I agree it will be difficult fitting this estate into the scheme of things. I can't live in two places at once so I'm going to have to give some thought to what is to be done. The war has taken many of the people who worked for my family in Sussex. If the war is indeed over, now the Royalists have been beaten, then I shall employ an efficient bailiff and a number of able assistants to run the estates. It will be a full-time job and the interests of the tenant farmers and production will be my prime concern.'

'You mean you will actually ride about the fields and supervise the work and inspect the ploughs like a menial,' she said, unable to resist teasing him.

'If I have to. I am not above hard work.'

She laughed, taking a swallow of her light ale. 'Then have a care. Your neighbours and fellow aristocrats will no doubt consider it unseemly and highly eccentric to see you labouring along with your workers.'

'And I will not care a fig what the gentry think, for the welfare of those who live and work the estates are important—which, I imagine, is how you see things.' There was a suggestion of mischief in his eyes. 'I do not see you as a defenceless female. A woman who has kept a castle and an estate running single-handedly for six years, who has gone through what you have and can still lift her head with spirit in her eyes is not one jot helpless—or defenceless. You are not afraid of getting your hands dirty when there are things to be done—however menial. Am I correct?'

'Yes, you are. Everyone has had to work extra hard over the past six years to get things done.' She looked into his eyes, trying to read his expression. There was a moment's silence and she discerned an admiration and a growing respect in his gaze.

'I salute your courage and your boldness, Catherine Stratton. You are undeniably brave, beautiful and one hell of a reckless woman.'

She gave him a grim look. 'Courage? Oh, no. Courage is something one finds when there is nothing left to fear. I haven't quite reached that point.'

His eyes softened. 'That's a cynical truth you've had to discover too early in your life.'

'Everything I have done has been sincere and there have been times when I risked everything to keep people safe when Parliamentary patrols came. Every step I have taken has been thought out and often agonised over for hours. But there have been many times, like today, when I could saddle my horse and take to the hills to put things into perspective and think about the future. Now I know that Thomas is dead I can think ahead. What kind of reception I will receive from my father I shall have to wait and see.' She raised her tankard. 'Let us hope for better things.'

'Speaking of taking to the hills...'

'Yes?'

'There's a picturesque lake up there. I thought you might have taken me.'

Catherine stared at him in horror. 'A lake... I...'

John chuckled softly at her confusion. 'Yes—it's one Thomas and I used to swim in often as boys.'

'You did?' She had a horrible idea where this was leading. There was a knowing, wicked gleam in his eyes.

'Do you ride up there often?'

'Yes—I mean—no—sometimes.'

'You did—yesterday morning.' He looked at her, his lips curved as he enjoyed her sudden confusion.

'Did I? Oh, yes—I remember.'

'Strange that I should have been there at the same time, yet we missed each other. Did you like what you saw, Catherine?' His voice was low, provocative.

Catherine flushed scarlet. 'No—I don't know. Do you normally go swimming in the middle of November? The water must have been freezing.'

'I swim at any time and anywhere when there is somewhere to swim. It's invigorating. You should try it some time.'

'But—you knew I was there?'

He nodded. 'Not at the time—otherwise I would have saved your blushes.'

'Then when?'

'When I heard you follow me back. I'm a soldier, trained to detect when I'm being followed. When I saw you ride into the courtyard, I knew it was you. Do you swim, Catherine?'

'No, I don't.'

He laughed out loud as the shock registered on her face. 'Worry not. I'm not in the least offended that you were watching me.' He turned to her, his face alight with humour. 'But if there is a next time, if you let me know you are there, I will teach you how to swim.'

She scowled at him. 'There won't be a next time. You're enjoying my discomfiture, aren't you?'

'Enormously.'

'You could have spared my feelings and done the gentlemanly thing by not mentioning the incident.'

'I could—but where's the fun in that? Now in which direction shall we ride next? To the lake, perhaps?'

'No. I've decided that the lake is off limits.'

* * *

Returning to their horses to begin their return journey to Carlton Bray, John took her arm as they crossed the yard. The fabric did nothing to lessen the warmth of his skin against hers. If anything, it added the awareness of sensuality she felt emanating between them. In that moment, when all her senses seemed to be heightened nearly beyond endurance, she knew she was more of a woman than she had ever been. Mentally, she was aware of her own growing maturity, experiencing all of a woman's physical needs and longings and desires for the first time in her life that could only be matched by one man—this man—John Stratton.

Her heart was touched by the warmth of the bond developing between them. She smiled softly as she was forced to acknowledge the pleasure that she found in his company and conversation and the disturbing sensations that heated her body when they were together.

Chapter Three

Catherine descended the stairs to the hall. No one looking at her would know how she gritted her teeth and steeled herself for the journey ahead, refusing to betray the trepidation she felt on reaching her destination and seeing her father for the first time in five years.

Conversation between John and Will Price ceased when she appeared. When she stepped into the range of John's vision, it was evident he could not believe the beautiful and well-groomed lady was the same young woman who had gone about the business of the castle in male garb. Attired in a dark green woollen dress with a white lace collar and a travelling cloak sitting loosely on her shoulders, her wonderful mane of golden hair arranged in a chignon at the back of her head and delightful curls flirting with her cheeks, she seemed the very spirit of virtue and moved with all the poise, grace and cool dignity of a queen.

She moved to stand close to John, tilting her head

as she gazed into his handsome visage from beneath eyebrows delicately sweeping like a winged bird. A bloom of rosy pink heightened her high cheekbones. The firelight gave her hair a rich warm hue and the faint scent of rosewater on her skin was intoxicating. A leisurely smile moved across John's face as his perusal swept her.

'You see, John,' she said, pulling on her kid gloves, 'I can look like a lady when I have a mind. I did consider riding all the way to London, but, should my stay turn out to be extensive, I must take enough clothes and things I might need while I am there. Unfortunately, I don't have a maid so I will have to make do. My baggage has been taken out to the coach so I am ready to leave when you are. I trust the escort we have riding with us are well armed. I should hate to be set upon at any time and rendered helpless by outlaws.'

'My dear Lady Stratton, when were you ever helpless?' John laughed. 'And God help any outlaw if they should dare attack you.'

Seeing the amusement in his wickedly dancing eyes and infuriating grin, she swallowed the flippant reply she might have given him and said instead, 'Have you broken your fast?'

John felt his pulse leap and the blood go searing through his veins at her nearness and the coyness of her little smile as she demurely lowered her eyes. He nodded. 'Will and I had breakfast together.'

'Good.' She shifted her gaze to the new steward of Carlton Bray who was taking on his new position with much enthusiasm. 'I think we have covered everything, Will, but anything else you need to know you only have to ask Miles.'

Trying not to show how sore her heart was at leaving Carlton Bray and all those who had depended on her since her marriage to Thomas, and swallowing down the constriction in her throat, she went out to the waiting coach. The four men who had accompanied John to act as escort were already mounted. Climbing inside the coach, Catherine sat arranging her skirts while John strode to his waiting horse. She watched and was not surprised when he hoisted himself into the saddle with ease and agility.

Daylight had just broken when the small party of riders and the large leather travelling coach with a domed roof left Carlton Bray Castle, heading east towards London. A grey mist swathed the land and hawthorn berries hung heavy in the hedgerows. Catherine had spent time instructing Will Price on the running of the estate and expressing her gratitude to him for being willing to take it on. She was confident that she was leaving matters in reliable hands and that he would manage it well.

The only view to be had of the passing countryside was to be seen out of the door, which had a leather curtain suspended from an iron bar, raised for the time being. Catherine was alone, her gaze never straying from the passing scenery which was familiar to her, having ridden the fields and byways many times. The poorly sprung coach rumbling and swaying over the uneven roads gradually lulled her senses and she closed her eyes, letting her thoughts take her where they would.

Well armed with swords and pistols, they had kept their eyes open for footpads and the like—desperate men had taken to the roads following the wars. Fortunately the first part of their journey had passed without mishap. When dusk began to fall they stopped at a coaching inn serving the needs of travellers for food, drink and rest. The men who accompanied them were happy to pass the evening in the main room while John ordered supper for himself and Catherine to be served in a small private parlour.

Other patrons were milling about and Catherine's gaze strayed to three women seated on a settle at an angle to the fire. They were young and pretty and made no attempt to conceal their attraction for John. They stared, openly appraising him, and Catherine saw how their eyes followed him with feminine interest and speculation. Aware of their interest, John returned their stare with bold and obvious pleasure. Smiling broadly, he bowed to them before taking Catherine's arm.

'Come,' he said. 'We'll dine in style—alone, I hope.'

'I'm flattered,' Catherine remarked. 'I admit to being quite ravenous, yet the idea of eating in the main body of the inn crammed with strangers is unappealing. I'll enjoy your company, John, but I'll understand if you'd prefer a more accommodating female companion.' She was unable to resist the impish response.

Her suggestion brought laughter to his lips. 'I'm no libertine, Catherine, and no Puritan either come to that—and I'd much rather dine with you by far.'

'Really? I'm flattered—but I did see how those ladies looked at you. You are a handsome man, John, and I am sure the ladies adore you.'

'Devil take it, Catherine! When this journey is over, how am I ever going to regard you as the lady of Carlton Bray again?'

'Oh, I think you'll manage very well.'

A fire warmed the room and the food which they ate in companionable silence was good. Feeling relaxed after the meal, the fatigue beginning to leave her bones and a tiredness wrapping itself around her, Catherine settled back in her chair, watching as John mopped up the last of the beef stew with a crust of bread.

'You have enjoyed your meal, John?' she asked as he drained his tankard of ale and set it down on the table.

Wrapped in the timeless lull that had fallen on him following the hot meal, the dim light of the parlour was filled with hazy shadows. Idly John gazed across the table at his companion with a good deal of pleasure, for she was a sight to heat any man's blood. Her low voice sent a thrill through him and he wanted nothing more than to reach across the table and pull her towards him and crush his mouth down on hers. With her face flushed to a soft pink glow and her eyes two sleepy orbs of emerald green, she was all temptation and he felt the blood pump rapidly through his body.

'I recall Thomas telling me about your home in Sussex, John.'

He nodded. 'Inglewood is where I grew up, along with my siblings. It was idyllic—and close to the sea. It was my mother's family home. I have acquired lands in the Midlands, but I chose to remain in Sussex. The loss of my father and Richard has thrust me to the head of the family, which was something I never aspired to.'

'And with it the title of Earl Fitzroy. How did that come about?'

'My maternal grandfather, Simon Fitzroy, acquired the title. The Fitzroys had always been gentry and although my grandfather had himself achieved an earldom by ability and assiduous attention to Queen Elizabeth and being in her favour, he had no real admiration for the aristocracy, not to mention Papists.'

'Then how did the estate pass to you?'

'The estate was not entailed and my grandfather was free to do with it as he liked. There was no one else so he passed the estate and title to his daughter's eldest child, Richard, where he felt it would be best served. Sadly, when Richard was killed at Edgehill, it passed to me. With Thomas's demise I seem to have inherited another title, that of Lord Stratton.'

'And your mother?'

'She is at home with my young sister, Elizabeth. I have two younger brothers—both married with children—one in Norfolk and the other in Kent.'

'And did they take part in the wars?'

'They both fought at various battles alongside my

father—they were more fortunate and returned home to their wives.'

'I'm sorry. What a terrible time it must have been for your mother—for all of you—to lose your father and a brother.'

'Many brave men died—on both sides.' He sighed, his expression one of melancholy. 'I have been so pre-occupied with the war of late—with fighting battles and keeping the soldiers in my regiment in order—that I have seen little of my family these past months. I will travel down to Sussex when I have delivered you to your father.'

His statement brought a smile to Catherine's lips. 'You make me sound like a parcel.'

He laughed, relaxed, stretching his long booted legs out in front of him. His eyes were warm as they met her gaze. 'It was not my intention to give offence.'

'None taken. How long do you think it will take us to reach London?' she asked, taking a sip of her wine.

He acknowledged her question with a bland smile, his eyelids dipping languidly over his dark eyes as he continued to study her at length, musing in rueful reflection over her predicament, for he knew how re-luctant she was to become reacquainted with her fa-ther. 'If we continue to make good time, the day after tomorrow. It is a long time since you saw your father. He is anxious to see you.'

'Just how ill is he, John? Do you think he has taken to his bed?'

'Probably. But he is not one to complain and the

mere fact that he stressed his wish to see you tells me his illness is more serious than he would have me know.'

'I wonder how Blanche is coping with his illness,' Catherine mused aloud. 'She does not have a caring disposition.'

'She will do her best, I imagine.'

'I believe the war has cost my father a great deal of money. He did very well for himself in the King's Customs House as a younger man. It was when he realised that, along with other families supportive of the King, he was expected to lend large sums to him with little expectation of a speedy return that he went over to Parliament. He accused the King of bleeding the country dry with excessive taxes and ignoring the advice of Parliament. He could not condone his plans to bring in outside assistance in the form of French troops— and, more damning than that, to bring over the Catholic Irish, promising them favours if they agreed to fight on his side.'

'You are right, Catherine. That would not have been tolerated. It resulted in the King's loss of popularity and prestige. Many Royalists gave up, many compounding with Parliament. Your father did the right thing when he opted to support Parliament.'

'That is your opinion. There are others who would agree with you,' she said, her face expressionless, which brought a narrowing to John's eyes as not for the first time he wondered at her allegiance. 'My father hoped Thomas would do the same, but Thomas was a staunch Royalist through and through—as you well know. I entered the marriage with reasonable resources. As my father's only offspring he saw to that. He has land in Berkshire that brings in a tidy sum. When things soured between him and Thomas, I know he regretted the marriage, especially when Thomas beggared himself, handing my dowry over to the King to help fund the war.'

John's interest was roused. 'And did you approve of him doing that?

'In so far as it left me with very little to sustain Castle Bray, no. Oft were the times when I wished I had more.'

'The wars have ruined many good families throughout the land. Its effects will be felt for years to come.'

'I agree with you. I am sure I will find everything much different in London. I seem to have been buried in the country without outside companionship for so long that I am out of touch, not only with the country, but my own family.'

'That may be so, but few women of my acquaintance would know how to run a castle as well as you have done. You were too young to be burdened with so much responsibility. It was an unexpected obligation you could have done without.'

Catherine felt a flush of pleasure rise to her cheeks at the unexpected praise. 'Yes, you could say that.' She responded to his obvious concern with more honesty than she might usually allow. 'I only did what had to be done—like any other woman would have done faced with the same situation. There was no one else.'

'Thomas loved Carlton Bray. He would have returned had he been able.'

'Yes, I believe he would. I am sure that if he had been taken prisoner I would have been told. Was it not the case that when officers were captured, on either side, it was normal for commanders to negotiate exchanges of officers of equivalent rank, that they could even be paroled on the promise never to fight again?'

'Yes, and you are right. If he had been captured, you would have been notified. As it turned out he simply pleased himself—spending time over the border and involving himself in one skirmish after another.'

'Thomas was not an easy man to live with. He hated it when I questioned his authority, his judgement.'

'He was like that. He was not noted for his patience and his temper could often get the better of him. Certainly you, as a sixteen-year-old girl, should not have been given in marriage to him.'

'I had no choice. I had to marry—as most women do. As a soldier, Father, who lived to fight the war against the King, almost forgot about his daughter tucked away on the Welsh border. Anxious to be rid of me, he forced me to marry a stranger. The thought of marriage and all it entailed was anathema to me. My father called it my duty. That was the moment I knew he didn't love me. But I knew in those early days that if I did not harden my heart he would destroy me.'

John realised that her marriage to his cousin had

hardened her heart not only against life, but against men in general, which was a terrible shame. Looking across at where she sat relaxed in her chair, her face flushed with the heat from the fire and the wine, for a moment he became locked in the spell of her dark, sultry eyes. He could not look away. She was like an innocent temptress, waiting for him, her chest rising and falling as if in anticipation of some excitement. It was not right that a gently reared girl, protected all her young life, should have been married to a stranger, virtually abandoned and exposed to such horror. He felt a deep anger burn inside him when he thought of Thomas's treatment of her.

'Had your mother been alive at the time, I assume she would not have sanctioned the marriage.'

'No, she would not. She would have been horrified at the prospect. Although it would not have made any difference. Father always got his own way. When my mother became ill, he didn't want her because she hadn't given him a son. Towards the end she cried a lot—not that she wanted me to know, but I would hear her sobbing in her room. I wanted passionately to be a boy. If I had been, everything would have been different.'

'Not necessarily. Life can be hard on men also.'

Catherine smiled indulgently. 'And only a man would say that. I suppose if Carlton Bray had been sequestered, if I could have found the money to pay the fine, it would have enabled me to keep it—not that it matters now it is yours.'

'You would not have been able to do that without Thomas's consent and he would never have asked for pardon for backing the King.'

'But you told me that it's all over for the King.'

'I believe it is, but the Royalists cannot simply pay a fine and beg pardon as if there's no harm done. And consider this. Would Thomas have wanted to return, to live under Parliament's rule when he fought so hard against it?'

'No—perhaps he would not. I'm just thankful that I know what happened to him. If I had never found out, my situation would have been dire indeed. I would have been forced to remain his wife for the rest of my life.'

'Not necessarily. After seven years and without sight or sound of him, you would be free of your vows and able to declare yourself a widow.'

'I would be free?' He nodded. 'Seven years?'

'That's the law.'

'I didn't know. So—since he has been missing for the past four years—after another three, I would have been able to declare myself a widow?'

'Yes—and you would be free to marry again if you so wished.'

Catherine grimaced. 'I cannot think of that now. Indeed, I cannot think of a man I would wish to marry— although I am sure my father will find me one if he has a mind.'

'I don't doubt it, not for one minute, but you are

of an age to make your own decisions and would be within your rights to defy your father.'

Catherine smiled. 'You make everything seem so simple. Think yourself fortunate that you are his friend and not his daughter.' Stifling a yawn, she got to her feet. 'I'm going to bed. I cannot believe how tired I feel when I have done little but sit in a carriage while it carried me along.'

John accompanied her to the door. 'If I could make things easier for you, I would,' he said softly, capturing her gaze. 'You have done your duty with good sense and remarkable courage.'

Catherine's eyes seemed to be caught by his. They conveyed strange things to her, stirring her instincts. He was smiling, but in his dark eyes a glow began, causing her to look away in confusion. Placing the tip of his finger beneath her chin, he turned her face back to his, his face becoming set in lines of smiling challenge. Her instinct told her she must go—yet John was set on delaying her. When he drew her close she had a feeling of helplessness and was aware of nothing else but his overwhelming presence. His eyes held a burning glow of intent, but deep in their depths there was something else she had never seen before, something that defied analysis and made her wary.

'You are a beautiful young woman, Catherine. Would you mind if I kissed you?'

She stared at him, not having expected this. 'A kiss?'

'Yes, a kiss, Catherine. Just a kiss. You might find it pleasurable,' he said, his eyes fastened on her trembling lips.

'But it won't be just a kiss, will it?'

'How can you know until you have sampled it?' Reaching out his hand, he caressed her cheek with featherlike fingertips. 'You tremble. Do you fear me?'

Panic seized her, but she was powerless to escape. She waited for the screaming denial to come from the dark recesses of her mind—of Thomas when he had forced himself on her. But she was determined to quell the intrusion and the trepidation that had arisen and surged within her. This wasn't Thomas. This was John and he was not forcing her as Thomas had done. He was awaiting her consent. The knowledge stilled her panic. When she met John's eyes, she knew she did not want to withdraw.

'It has nothing to do with fear.'

He drew his finger gently down the bare flesh of her slender neck. 'Then kiss me, Catherine. Just a kiss.' His expression softened. He seemed to understand more of what was going on in her mind than she had thought. 'I am not Thomas. I am nothing like him. You will not find kissing me either distasteful or undignified. I will not hurt you. This I promise you.'

He drew her closer, his face poised close to hers, looking deep into her eyes, his warm breath caressing her face. Lowering his head, he covered her mouth with his own, his lips at first gentle before becoming more insistent, parting her own and kissing her slowly, long and deep. She strained to resist the feel of his hands on her body, his mouth on hers, but her weak flesh began to respond and at last she yielded, her lips answering his in mindless rapture.

She became languid and relaxed with sensuality, uttering a moan and a sigh of pleasure. Sensations like tight buds opened and exploded into flowers of splendour, growing stronger and sweeter. His kiss was deep and endless, one that shook her to the core of her being and made her want more. His lips courted hers with a fierce tenderness, moving over them with accomplished persuasion, tasting their sweetness, coaxing them to part, his tongue making a brief, sensuous exploration of the soft warmth within.

Lost in a sea of pure, blossoming sensation, she moaned softly. She felt the hardness of his body pressed close to her own and a melting softness flowed through her veins, evoking feelings she had never experienced before or thought herself capable of feeling. Only one man had touched her in intimacy—Thomas—but his lovemaking had been clumsy and brutal, giving no thought to pleasuring her.

All too soon he withdrew his lips and she caught her breath, gasping, when he buried them in the soft pulsating curve of her throat, before finding her mouth once more. Sliding her hands up his hard chest, she let them rest on either side of his neck, pressing herself closer, feeling the strength in that hard, lean body.

When he raised his head she felt it strange that she did not fear the way he was looking at her—quite the

opposite, in fact, for she found herself unprepared for
the sheer force of the feelings that swept through her
and knew that she was in grave danger, not from John,
but from herself. The prospect of letting him kiss her
once more seemed not only harmless but irresistibly
appealing and she was tempted to repeat the action,
but something deep inside stopped her.

As if sensing a change in her, John pulled back.
The rigid set of her shoulders discouraged further in-
timacies.

'Good Lord! You are exquisite,' he murmured hus-
kily. 'But I can see I've shocked you.'

It was true, he had, but Catherine was more shocked
at herself and her own reaction than anything he had
done. 'Yes. This is madness. I must go,' she whispered,
shocked by the force of her feelings. 'This should not
be happening. You should not be doing this. We should
not… It is wrong.' Turning from him, she left, hitch-
ing up her skirts and climbing the stairs to the chamber allotted to her.

John stood and watched her go, having wanted more
of her. Hearing her soft moan and her faint inhalation
when his lips had caressed hers, he had been satisfied and encouraged by her reaction. Purposefully he
had tightened his embrace, feeling her body shudder
against his, and he had realised with a surge of desire
that her demureness and reserve hid a woman of intense passion. Catherine possessed an indescribable
magnetism in abundance, with that unique quality of

innocence and sexuality rarely come by. She was a woman with a combination of youthful beauty and an untouched air of shy modesty—despite her marriage to Thomas—yet she had about her a well-bred quality. When she smiled a small dimple appeared in her cheek and her rosy parted lips revealed perfect, small white teeth.

John was enchanted. He thought he had never seen anything quite so appealing or irresistibly captivating as Catherine Stratton. Women like her were as scarce as a rare jewel and must be treated as such, and he was determined that she would not escape him. He wanted her, wanted to fill his mouth with the taste of her, to have those inviting hips beneath him, to have those long, lithe legs wrapped around him.

He thought of the last words she had uttered, that what they had done was wrong. He knew that as well as she did. He should not be harbouring any kind of romantic thoughts about her and knew very well that he should not kiss her again.

With the noise of the inn below, Catherine climbed into bed, hoping that sleep would soon claim her. But her head was too full of the day's events and what would be waiting for her when she reached London. Thoughts of John soon invaded her mind and she was shocked by the force of her feelings. She closed her eyes tight in an attempt to banish his face from her mind, but she could not banish the essence of the warm animal magnetism that had filled her when they were together, when his lips had kissed hers. When her eyes had flickered open his lean and handsome features had been starkly etched. A strange feeling, until that moment unknown to her, had fluttered within her breast and a flood of excitement had surged through her.

Her face became soft and wistful as she stared at the shadows created by a solitary candle burning on a table by the window. Her arms hugged her slender waist, as if they sought to simulate a lover's embrace, which was but a memory of their kiss. Breathing deep and closing her eyes, she felt again the ache in her breasts when they had been crushed against John's hard chest and the warmth of his breath against her lips.

She felt bemused, utterly and completely bewildered by her feelings, by her emotions, which made her so unsure of herself. What was the matter with her that she should desire the embrace of a man who had not appeared in her life until three days ago? Why was she so conflicted? And how different he was from Thomas. She had been Thomas's wife and had found no softening in her heart for him, yet now her mind envisioned the dark, handsome face of the man who had taken her from Carlton Bray.

Thomas's rough, careless handling of her when he had taken her to his bed had left her scarred, this she knew, but since she had met John, ever since she met the flesh and bone of the man, she had felt there was more to it than she could ever have imagined. When John had taken her in his arms he had aroused feelings inside her in the most startling way. She did wonder

what her life would have been like had she married
John instead of Thomas. As soon as the thought took
hold she reproached herself. She told herself firmly
that she was no starry-eyed girl. She was cautious now.
Wiser. It would not do to think along those lines. To
show emotion was a weakness and if she was to avoid
putting herself in the power of John Stratton it was
imperative that she kept her feelings closed at all cost.

The following morning—Catherine having slept
so badly from her lumpy mattress and feeling so little rested that she was up before cockcrow—they left
the inn as soon as they had eaten. The rain which had
been falling for most of the night ceased as the coach
pulled out of the inn yard. The sun broke through the
clouds and sent them scudding back to the east, giving
way to a huge sweeping canvas of blue sky. In order
to make good time, they travelled at speed, stopping
only for the briefest of meals and to rest the horses.

Alone for long hours inside the coach, her eyes were
constantly drawn to John when he rode alongside. An
unaccustomed warmth stole through her when she remembered their embrace of the night before, the awareness of her body coming alive beneath the caressing
boldness of his lips and the pleasure this had given her,
making her aware of her own body's weakness and
its readiness to betray everything she fought against.
Sensing her watching him, he would meet her gaze
boldly. His own held a silent challenge, seeming to
possess a keen ability to know the reason for the con-

fusion which would swamp her at times and cause her to flush crimson like a young girl and avert her gaze.

It was when they took respite from the journey that John found himself alone with Catherine. She was outside the inn, sitting on a low wall, her woollen cloak drawn close about her, waiting for their journey to resume. He sensed that what they had done the night before continued to concern her and he could not blame her. He was astounded to discover how close he had come to losing control. Catherine affected him deeply. Her openness drew a whole new response from him and, after many years of war and riding from one end of the country to the other, he felt a peculiar kind of freedom that was entirely new to him, a process that had begun when a woman attired in breeches had walked into his life. But from the very beginning he had vowed that his emotions would not become involved. She was newly widowed. He could not make her the instrument of his desire.

Sitting beside her, he turned towards her. 'I want to apologise for my behaviour last night, Catherine. You were right. It was madness and not what I intended. I think we let the moment get the better of us.'

'Yes, I think so. You took a liberty. Do you make a habit of kissing recently widowed ladies?'

'Not usually,' he said, taking her hand and contemplating her slender fingers, relieved that she did not snatch it away. 'In truth, you are the first—and the last, I expect. It was a mistake. If it were to happen

again, it would spoil something that I value highly—
our friendship. I respect you and your privacy, yet I
realise that what I want to do offends against both of
us. We neither of us conform to what convention de-
mands. Freedom, no encumbrances, clearly appeals to
us both.' He kept an edge to his voice, but his expression revealed nothing of his thoughts and his eyes were
carefully guarded. 'That must not happen, not when
we are soon to part.'

'No, it must not.'

John sighed heavily, seeing her fine-boned profile
expressionless as she stared straight ahead before she
turned her head and her clear green eyes held his own.
He had known no other like her and could not help
but wonder at the grit of her. 'You are a courageous
woman, Catherine. I feel deeply the burden of your
present predicament and I am concerned about you. I
feel that despite your outward show of bravado, you
need protection.'

'Thank you, John, but you needn't feel under any
obligation. Do not be anxious on my account. If I can
survive the ordeal of the past four years at Carlton
Bray, I can survive most things.'

'I made my assessment regarding your success at
doing that the first day we met. You have developed
a strength and independence that is a rarity indeed in
the women of my acquaintance.'

She smiled, looking down at her hand still held in
his. 'I suddenly realised that, were we to have remained
longer at Carlton Bray, I would be in danger of becom-

ing too dependent on you. The aftermath of the terrible days when the castle became the focus of Parliament forces had left me feeling cast adrift and it was too easy to surrender to your embrace.

'It wouldn't have been at all difficult to carry on kissing you, but you are right. It would be best not to do anything to destroy our friendship—although I cannot deny that I enjoyed the kiss.' She tipped back her head and laughed, her eyes alight with mischief. 'I doubt I would raise any objections if you were to re-peat what you deem to be an offence against us both.'

She faced him, slender and proud, and when she laughed like that John caught his breath at the prom-ise she gave of unfettered, vibrant woman. His mouth quirked in a half-smile as his heavy-lidded gaze dropped to her soft lips, lingering hungrily on her mouth.

Suddenly his face became sombre. He continued to hold her hand. Catherine looked at him, sensing a change in him. 'John? What is it? You look very seri-ous all of a sudden. Is something wrong?'

He shook his head. 'No—at least, I hope not. There is something I think you should know before we reach Oakdene, something your father should have told you, but I suspect, for reasons of his own, he has omit-ted to do so.' He wanted to tell her the truth, wanting not to hurt her while knowing she would be when he disclosed what had been quietly troubling him since meeting her.

A coldness entered Catherine's veins and something crawled along her spine, touching an instinct, a premonition of impending disaster. 'Tell me. What is it, John?'

'Blanche gave birth to a child, James, three years ago. The fact that you haven't mentioned him tells me that you are ignorant of the fact.'

Feeling as if the breath had been knocked from her body, rendered silent, she looked at him with blind incredulity. 'I am. A—a child—my brother?' What she felt brought a stabbing pain to her heart and tears sprang to her eyes. She had a brother—a half-brother—and no one had bothered to tell her. 'I see. It shouldn't be such a surprise discovering that Blanche has a son, but why have they kept it from me?'

'It was not my place to tell you, but I am of the opinion that you should know. It will be less of a shock when you arrive at Oakdene if you know about it. Your father should have written to you to tell you the happy news.'

'He did write—four years too late and summoning me to London, with not a mention of a son. Have you seen him—James?'

'No. Whenever I've been at Oakdene he was secreted away in the nursery.'

'Father should have told me. He must have known that I would find out eventually. Thank you for telling me, John.'

'People take different views on things like that. After the past years of strife I suppose there are those who think it's better to get through life as easily as one

can—and if ignorance is more soothing than knowledge, then let us remain in the dark.'

'That is a strange philosophy. Do you approve?'

'Clearly not, otherwise I would not have told you.
But I am sure there are many things you have opinions about, Catherine, and my approval or disapproval
is not one of them.'

The moment was interrupted by the coach driver
waving to them, indicating that they were ready to
move on. John released her hand and they stood up.

'Come. We have a journey to finish.'

Mounting his horse, John felt a deep, unutterable
sadness. The pain inside Catherine must be terrible
and for the first time since he had known her father,
Edward Kingsley, he felt anger towards him for ignoring his beautiful daughter for most of her life.

For the rest of the journey, preferring not to dwell
on the news he had just imparted, but on the evening
before when he had held Catherine in his arms, John
derived immense pleasure from the memory he carried with him. Not even the succulent meal he had
devoured at the landlord's table before their departure could compete with the comeliness of Catherine's
adorable assets. On a more serious note, he knew he
must fight to keep tight rein on his desire where she
was concerned. He was in no position to form any
kind of relationship with her until the outcome of what
he knew was waiting for her at Oakdene House had
been resolved.

Chapter Four

Catherine sat in the gloom of the coach, the shafts of winter light through the small window reflecting her mood. Everything outside was muted as though to match the feeling in her. She tried to feel pleased that she had a sibling, but she was terribly hurt and disappointed that no one had thought to tell her about him.

The air was filled with an early winter chill as they passed under the gatehouse into the well-maintained grounds of Oakdene House, a mile south-west of London. A wide avenue of stately oaks led to the house. Built in warm red brick, its lines pure and simple, with tall lead-paned windows, the sight brought a hard lump of emotion to Catherine's throat. Her gaze swept over the exquisite gardens which her mother had loved so much. They consisted of green lawns and clipped box hedges, of flowering shrubs and trees with variegated leaves and a charming little summer house.

The coach pulled up in front of the house, the horses steaming from their exertions. Her heart beating in hard thuds of trepidation, Catherine climbed out. The massive oak door was opened by a male servant she did not recognise. The loyal staff who had served the Kingsleys over the years had dwindled somewhat since she had left, but some of the faces she would recognise.

As she stepped into the wainscoted hall with its gleaming parquet floor, the years she had been absent were rolled away. She had not been back since her marriage to Thomas, but everything was still the same. The large hall was panelled in oak and a carved staircase rose to the upper floors.

Dressed in a gown of sombre black, Mrs Coleman, the housekeeper who had been at Oakdene for as long as Catherine could remember and who was expecting her, came forward to welcome her home. There was a bright, cheery smile on her round face and tears of gladness in her eyes. She was a pleasant, capable woman, elderly now and smelling faintly of lavender water, but still able to run the household efficiently.

'It's so good to see you back after all this time, my lady,' she said, bobbing a curtsy. A plain collar and cuffs relieved the stark black of her gown and on her white hair was a white cap, the keys of the house hanging heavily from her waist.

'It's good to be back, Mrs Coleman. It's been a long time. You are well, I hope.'

'I am—apart from a few aches and pains which are to be expected at my age. I must tell you how eagerly we have all awaited your coming.'

'Thank you, Mrs Coleman. That's reassuring to know.'

Mrs Coleman stepped back when a door opened and her stepmother swept into the hall. Catherine's heart sank. Blanche was not old enough to be her mother. Only eight years separated them in age, but there was a vast difference between them in temperament and form. Blanche was shorter in stature compared to her stepdaughter and more voluptuous. She was also outspoken and had delighted in undermining Catherine and taking her to task over something or other when she had married her father and come to live at Oakdene House. In fact, living in the same house together before Catherine had married Thomas, she had constantly made life downright unpleasant for her and a wall of antipathy had sprung up between them.

With dark brown hair, flashing brown eyes and full red lips, Blanche was a handsome woman. She carried a certain elegance and charm, but a coarseness in her manner and her eyes betrayed the truth of her nature. They were small and calculating, deep and dangerous and ever watchful. She was such an overpowering person that most people felt subdued in her presence, but Catherine refused to be put down by her domineering manner.

She might be the wife of a Parliamentary man, but, attired in dark blue velvet with a fine lace collar and cuffs, she was by no means a Puritan. Her appearance was benevolent and smiling, but Catherine was not deceived. She offered no words of welcome—Catherine did not expect it. The arrogance in her demeanour was not diminished by the many years they had been apart. She managed a faint inclination of her elegantly coifed head and a frosty smile, before settling her austere gaze on her in a cool and exacting way. Impersonally her eyes raked Catherine with the cold, speculating expression of a long-standing opponent.

'So, you have come back,' she commented wryly and with a practised smile, giving Catherine a flash of sharp white teeth from between her parted lips.

There were hidden connotations behind that smile and Catherine was not quite sure how to read them, but whether meant to insult or compliment, the two of them were to live in this house for as long as Catherine remained in London and it would not do to be constantly at daggers drawn. There was nothing like a smile to confuse a foe or charm a friend and Catherine's lips curved graciously.

'As you see, Blanche,' she replied pleasantly, slipping the cloak from her shoulders and handing it to the servant who had opened the door to them.

'Do you intend to stay long?'

'As long as my father needs me. How is he?'

Blanche gave her an arch look. 'He is very ill. The journey from Newcastle was too much for him and he is confined to his bed for most of the day. I do not want him upset.'

If Blanche hoped to see a flicker of emotion pass across Catherine's face, she was disappointed, for, used to Blanche's barbed comments, Catherine's expression remained unchanged.

'Of course not. I assure you I have no intention of upsetting him. He sent for me. Now, if you don't mind, I will go and see him.'

'Later, perhaps. The physician came to see him this morning and the visit exhausted him. He's sleeping at present—which he does for most of the day.'

Catherine studied her through narrowed eyes. Having no wish to start any battles, though it grieved her not to see her father just now, this was one time she would concede. 'I see, then I will see him later.'

'Yes, that would be best.' She looked beyond Catherine when the door opened and John stepped into the hall. Bestowing her most dazzling smile on him, she stepped round Catherine and went to greet him.

Catherine turned to Mrs Coleman. 'Has my old room been made ready, Mrs Coleman?'

'It has. I'm sure you would like to change after your long and tiring journey. I'll have some hot water sent up.'

'Thank you. I would appreciate that.' When the elderly woman would have proceeded her, Catherine stopped her. 'There's no need to come with me. I know the way to my own chamber.'

Catherine picked up her skirts and let out a long sigh as she mounted the stairs, aware that this was the way an encounter with Blanche had often left her in the past. They were at loggerheads most of the time, which was why she always avoided her company. The sound of Blanche's tinkling laughter drifted up to her from below and echoed along the landing with merciless mockery.

Memories of her childhood came flooding back when she opened the door and stepped inside her old room. Everything was just the same—the big tester bed and hangings. A fire burned in the fireplace, adding a warm glow to everything. Going to the bed, she ran her hand down the rich fabric of the hangings and, with a heavy sigh, went and sat on the cushioned window seat looking out over the gardens. For a moment it was as if time stood still and she was a child again, hearing her mother calling her name.

She remained where she was until water was brought up by a maid who said her name was Molly. She was pretty and pleasant and eager to please and told her the mistress had instructed her to be her maid for the duration of Lady Stratton's stay.

Catherine felt her heart sink when just before supper Blanche came to her room. Having finished her ablutions, she had wrapped her robe around her as she contemplated the gown she had chosen to wear for the early evening meal. She faced her stepmother with unflinching poise under her penetrating inspection.

'I thought I would come and welcome you properly, Catherine,' she said haughtily. 'I trust you find your room to your approval. I've tried many times to have it updated, but your father insisted it was to be left as it is.'

Catherine was surprised to hear this. She would not have thought her father cared one way or the other or had given any thought to so trivial a matter. 'It is just as I remember it, Blanche.' She went to sit at the dressing table, putting the small items she had brought with her necessary for her toilet in order. If Blanche had hoped to see a flicker of unease on her face, she would be disappointed.

'You look very grand this evening, Blanche,' Catherine said generously, looking at her through the mirror. Blanche had chosen to wear a gown of deep red, even though the colour accentuated the sharp angles of her face and scraped-back hair.

Blanche smiled. 'It's a rarity for us to have visitors these days. I have to dress for the occasion. You have changed, Catherine. The Welsh Marches seem to agree with you.'

Blanche's smile was condescending. Catherine was in no doubt that her stepmother had been convinced she would still be the same plain, meek girl who had married Thomas six years ago and her new-found confidence had somewhat blunted her attack. She would be disappointed and surprised that this assured woman was no longer a graceless chit.

'Yes, I was not disappointed—even though Thomas left to fight the war for the King almost immediately, so our marriage did not get off to an agreeable start, I'm afraid.'

'Perhaps that's because your marriage wasn't a love

match,' Blanche said, getting straight to the point. 'From the very beginning I knew he could never love you.'

Catherine smiled, not in the least shocked by Blanche's statement. 'Or I him. And why do you think that was, Blanche? Because he was in love with you? But you could not marry him, could you, because you were already married to my father. You encouraged my marriage to Thomas in order to keep him close, I know that.'

'You knew—you knew it was me he loved?' Blanche said, astonished and infuriated by Catherine's calm, cool manner.

'Yes, I knew. How could I not? You made eyes at him whenever he came to the house.'

Blanche's eyebrows raised as she stared across at Catherine, her lips twisting scornfully. 'You appear to have got over it. But you are right. Thomas would have married me had I not been married to Edward. The war kept us apart, but then when your fool of a father expressed his wish for you to marry, I realised it was just what I needed—what Thomas and I needed—a silly girl to marry off. It was child's play for Thomas to win your father over and persuade him to consider him for your husband—wealthy, titled and with a fine estate. It all worked out better than we could have hoped. You would be tucked away on the Welsh border while Thomas spent a great deal of his time in London—with me.'

Catherine favoured her with a cool, level stare, seeing at last the cynical calculation of which she had been the object and the cold-blooded way in which Blanche and Thomas had played on her innocence. 'What a scheming woman you are, Blanche. And my father had no idea—or did he? Unfortunately for you, you did not enjoy Thomas's favours for long, did you? How it must have galled you when the war intervened and my father went over to Parliament, distancing himself from Thomas—and me. When he went missing at Marston Moor in forty-four it must have come as more of a shock to you than it did to me. For myself I blessed my good fortune that he was gone from my life—if not permanently, then at least for a while. As things turned out, he died anyway of wounds he acquired in the struggle.'

'You could say that,' Blanche said quietly, averting her eyes and going to the door, as if the manner of Thomas's death and the pain it had caused her was too much for her to contemplate.

Catherine looked at her in exasperation. 'Why do you dislike me so much, Blanche? I was hoping that after all this time things would be improved between us.' When Blanche turned and looked at her Catherine saw her hesitate and bite her lip, unused to such directness from other people, despite her own rudeness.

'It may surprise you to know, Catherine, that I don't dislike you. I have no particular feelings about you at all.'

'Don't you? Then while I am here, at least tolerate me. I didn't choose to marry Thomas. Nor did I wish for his death. I didn't choose to spend the past four years of my life defending a fortress on the Welsh Marches either—often at the risk of my life while my husband was off fighting a war. I wasn't sitting idle. We both have our crosses to bear.'

Blanche had the grace to look embarrassed at the raw emotion in Catherine's voice and Catherine knew this was because she rarely met with opposition and that she should have spoken out before. It was high time she asserted herself where Blanche was concerned. If only Blanche had been more friendly towards her in the beginning, her life would have been more pleasant.

'Well, we both know he won't be coming back—and you can thank your father for that.'

Catherine detected a hint of sadness in her stepmother's eyes and her voice had softened. If Blanche had loved Thomas, then of course she would mourn his passing, which would have to be done in silence. 'Would you mind telling me what you mean by that, Blanche? What had my father to do with Thomas's passing? Is there something you know that I don't? If so, will you please tell me? I don't like secrets.'

Avoiding Catherine's eyes, Blanche got to her feet. 'No,' she said quietly, averting her eyes. 'It is nothing.'

Catherine wasn't so sure about that, but she did not pursue the issue.

'You grew to loathe Thomas, didn't you? It wasn't enough for you to bear his name, to be his wife—to serve him…'

'Serve him? I did not serve him,' Catherine retorted

scornfully, getting to her feet, refusing to be intimidated by such cutting remarks. 'I serve no man. I could not forgive his betrayal. Neither did I feel any affection for him. The thought of him touching me and demanding his rights filled me with revulsion. You were welcome to him.' She went to the bed and picked up the gown she had chosen to wear for supper. 'Now if you don't mind, Blanche, I would like to get dressed. I will see you at supper. Oh, and I would dearly like to see James.' When Blanche cast her a surprised look, Catherine smiled thinly. 'My father neglected to inform me of his birth. John told me.'

'I see. Yes—you can see him, but not tonight. And please do not mention the child in the presence of your father. He—he is not what he was and a young child agitates him. It is not good for him to get upset.'

Catherine frowned. 'I am sorry to hear that. I have no wish to upset him so I will do as you ask and look forward to seeing James tomorrow.'

'Thank you. I would appreciate that.'

Without another word Blanche left, leaving Catherine with a distinct feeling of unease. Why would it upset her father to discuss his son? Was it not what he had always wanted? And what had Blanche meant about her father having something to do with Thomas's demise? On a sigh she shook her head. No doubt she would find out in time.

In no hurry to confront Blanche again so soon, Catherine took her time with her toilet, choosing to wear an extremely fetching dark blue velvet gown which emphasised the slimness of her waist. It was a long time since she had taken such care with her appearance, but she'd had no occasion to do so at Carlton Bray. She even let Molly dress her hair in soft, high curls. When she felt confident that she looked her best, she went downstairs to the dining parlour. Taking a moment she paused, hearing a murmur of voices from inside.

Opening the door, she stepped inside. John was standing before the giant hearth where a fire burned bright, the lively flames sending dancing shadows over the richly tapestried walls lit by several wall tapers. There was no sign of Blanche. She was surprised to see her father ensconced in a large armchair beside the hearth, his feet resting on a footstool. He held all her attention, for she had not expected him to be well enough to dine with them. Conversation between the two men ceased when she made her entrance.

Catherine's gaze settled on John as she closed the door and walked towards them. He was watching her entrance like a large, predatory hawk, his wineglass arrested halfway to his lips. He had changed his clothes and looked extremely handsome and dignified in dark breeches and a tanned jerkin with a slash of white collar at his neck. His dark hair had been brushed to merciless neatness and drawn back to his nape where it was secured. There was a restlessness about him and she sensed he would feel more at ease outdoors than confined to the house. Switching her gaze to her father, she crossed to him and dropped a small curtsy.

'Father, I'm glad you are able to dine with us. I would have presented myself to you earlier, but Blanche told me you were resting. You have been ill. How are you now?'

She did not embrace him or show undue affection. He did not expect it and nor would he welcome it. To show any kind of affection or emotion he considered a weakness. Tension tightened her throat suddenly and a stone settled on her heart. Already she was wishing she had never left Carlton Bray. He did indeed look ill. Once so imposing a soldier in both bearing and training, he was now a mere shadow of the man who had earned a name for his military prowess in the service of Parliament. His body might suffer the ravages of ill health, but his mind was still active and intelligent and retained its instinct for command. His face was shrunken and thin, his white hair sparse, but the eyes that looked at her were still penetratingly sharp.

'No better,' he replied in answer to her question. His voice was low and rasped in his throat and he seemed to find it difficult to breathe. His stare was uncomfortably forthright and assessing. She smiled, but he did not return it. Her presence did not move him, neither did the tenuous link of kinship.

'You should have stayed in your chamber. I would have come to see you there.'

'While I am able to get downstairs I will continue to

do so. You made good time. I wondered if you would come.'

'You summoned me. How could I not?'

'We have not met since the early years of your marriage.'

'No—when you came to Carlton Bray to persuade Thomas to change his allegiance.'

'Which was a vain hope, but I tried.' Edward glanced up at John. 'You came quickly, John. I am grateful. It's good to see you, albeit in such circumstances—which are dire.' To his daughter, he said, 'So, Catherine, you are a widow.'

'Yes. I had not seen Thomas for some considerable time—four years, in fact.'

'Aye—Marston Moor. What a terrible battle that was—the worst. It was a victory for Parliament, but when I remember the suffering and the misery of it, it was a hollow victory. An enormous loss of so many courageous men—on both sides—including John's father. How are things at Carlton Bray? You managed without Thomas?'

'I did my best. It was not always easy.'

'Not if Thomas gave all his money to fund the King,' Edward grumbled. 'You haven't come to ask for money, I hope.'

'No, Father,' Catherine replied quietly, fighting back her disappointment. Any hopes she had harboured that he might have changed during the time they had been apart were shattered. He was still the same unfeeling man he had always been, with not one ounce of love or kindness for her. 'I have already told you that I came because you summoned me. I don't want your charity.'

'Good, because you won't get it from me. Not one penny piece will go to the upkeep of that damned castle.'

Catherine caught John's eye and said, 'The problem is no longer mine, Father. John is now the new Lord Stratton, owner of Carlton Bray Castle. I'm sure he will oversee the running of the estate splendidly.'

Her father's gaze went past her when the door opened. 'Sit and have your meal. We will talk at length tomorrow.'

Catherine didn't have time to reply, for at that moment Blanche walked in, positively glowing, supremely confident in her beauty, impeccably groomed and faultlessly attired. She was followed by servants carrying platters of steaming food and setting them on the table.

'Can I help you to the table, Father?'

'Edward will eat in his room,' Blanche said, crossing to the table to inspect the food.

His wife's high-handed manner brought a flash of anger to her husband's face, but it was gone as soon as it appeared. 'Tonight is an exception. We have guests. I will join you at the table.'

Blanche stopped what she was doing and cast him a look of impatience. 'Very well, Edward. If you think you are up to it, then of course you must.' She gestured to one of the servants. 'Help him, will you, Robert.'

It was a slow process, but between them John and Robert saw him seated at the head of the table. Blanche shot him a look bordering on hatred—which did not go unnoticed by Catherine—and virtually ignored him for the time it took them to eat the meal. He did not eat, but he had a glass of watered-down wine which he sipped.

Supper was a good meal of chicken broth, mutton steaks and roast ducks. The dining parlour glowed from the lighted tapers and the huge log fire in the hearth.

'Have you any news of the King?' Edward enquired of John. 'The last I heard he was being held prisoner on the Isle of Wight.'

'It is expected that he will be brought back to London to stand trial. He must be made to answer for his actions. He must also be made to swear never again to raise an army inside the kingdom. Parliament and the army will stand for nothing less.'

'But—on what charge?' Catherine asked.

'Treason.'

'But he is the King of England. No King of England has ever answered to law.'

'Not any more,' John said. 'His extravagance and callous disregard of our laws, his smug assumption of the divine right of his kingship, led us into disaster. There are many who want to see him answer for his crimes—for splitting the nation in two.'

'What of you, John?' Edward asked. 'I know you have matters of importance to take care of at Windsor, but you are more than welcome to remain here with us. Confined to the house as I've become, it's always good to catch up with news of the outside world.'

'Thank you, Edward. I would be grateful, although there will be nights when I must be at Windsor. The men who rode with us from Carlton Bray have gone to the army garrison there.'

'Of course, you must stay here,' Blanche said. 'Windsor is not far away if duty calls you, but it will not provide you with the comforts we can offer—and I know Edward would be glad of your company. And what of you?' she said, turning her attention to Catherine. 'You mentioned how there have been a few skirmishes in the Welsh Marches. I have to say you appear to have survived everything remarkably well.'

'Yes, as you see, Blanche.'

'Still, it's hardly woman's work, defending a fortress the size of Carlton Bray. Do you still wear breeches when you go about your work?' she asked with an underlying mockery, helping herself to more mutton.

'All the time. I find I am on and off my horse most of the time. Breeches are far more serviceable than skirts. You should try wearing them when you go riding— Oh, pardon me. I quite forgot. You don't ride, do you, Blanche?' She spoke flippantly, looking directly at Blanche, her eyes reminding her stepmother once more that she was no longer the green girl who had married Thomas, that she had seen and done too much to be either threatened or cowed. She was granted the satisfaction of seeing Blanche's poise waver before her merciless, bright young eyes.

Blanche's eyes did a quick sweep of Catherine's pale face and slender shape and she grimaced. 'Goodness me, I certainly do not! I'm not partial to horses—smelly things, I always think. But you really should take more care of yourself, Catherine.'

'I do, all the time, Blanche—as you see,' Catherine was quick to protest at the insufferable remark, but John gave an easy laugh.

'You would not be willing to wear breeches, Blanche?'

'No, I most certainly would not. I can't imagine anything more unfeminine. Now you find yourself a widow, Catherine, you will never get another man to wed you if you don't care what you look like.'

Catherine threw her a cold look, heedful of her father's eyes on her, assessing, judging, but thankfully not reproaching. 'Heaven forbid! The last thing I want in my life is another husband. Thomas did not exactly endear me to the institution of marriage. Why would I want to put myself through that again? I set my own course when he failed to come back from Marston Moor.'

Blanche raised her chin haughtily. 'What good will that do you? One cannot escape the fact that a woman with opinions such as those is enough to scare away certain gentlemen and as a result the lady—be she a widow or a spinster—will remain so until the day she dies.'

Catherine suppressed a smile. 'Oh, dear,' she said in a moment of sheer mischief. 'Now, that is a daunting prospect for any woman. You make securing a husband sound like a holy crusade for all women, Blanche.

Now that I find myself a widow, I have no intention of breaking one of my cardinal rules.'

'And that is?' Blanche enquired reluctantly.

'Never to consider a proposal of marriage unless the gentleman shares the same opinions and view as myself. We must be equal in all things. As a woman alone, for too long I've had people dependent on me, looking to me to make decisions, and when I did, praying they were the right ones. Which is why I refuse to dance attendance like a witless fool on any man who will expect me to submit to his authority and not to say anything other than yes and no, a man who will list me among his possessions, like his dogs and horses. I consider ideas such as these unacceptable and insulting.'

'You are rather harsh on the male sex, Catherine,' John remarked.

She glanced at him directly. He lounged back in his chair, his arm stretched across the back, his hand idly turning the silver wine goblet in his fingers. His expression was thoughtful as he listened with interest to what she had to say. 'It was not my intention to give offence.'

'None taken,' he said, smiling, 'but you have just damaged my ego beyond recall. How about you, Edward?'

'I think what my daughter was trying to say is that she has no intention of being owned by any man. Is that not so, Catherine?'

'Yes, Father.' She held his gaze, defiant but respectful. 'That is exactly what I meant. Although I must make it quite plain that I believe it is a wife's duty to be an asset to her husband in every way, but that there must be respect and consideration on both sides.'

'It sounds quite mad to me,' Blanche quipped.

'Sane, I think,' John countered, an amused glint in his eye.

'I don't doubt her sanity, John. It is simply that with ideas such as those, a woman is in danger of becoming eccentric and developing undesirable characteristics.'

'If you mean she is capable of taking care of herself, then I admire her for it.'

'You do? I am surprised. Were Thomas still alive I am sure Catherine would have cause to eat her words. He was not a man to be gainsaid.'

'And you would know that, would you, Blanche?' Unable to suppress a smile, Catherine glanced across the table at John. Having listened to the altercation between herself and Blanche, his face was a pleasantly smiling mask that hid all thoughts. But she was certain the glint that flashed into his eyes was one of congratulatory triumph.

Later, when her father had been taken to his room and the house was quiet, Catherine donned her cloak, too restless to think of sleep. Perhaps it was her unpleasant altercation with Blanche that made her so wide awake, or her meeting with her father, but she knew sleep wouldn't come just yet. With a walk on the battlements at Carlton Bray denied her, a walk in the garden would have to suffice.

Stars blazed in the dark sky like diamonds against black velvet and the full moon shone brightly over the gardens, while a cool breeze caressed her skin and stirred her hair. She had removed the pins and it hung in soft waves about her shoulders. Walking slowly along the winding paths, she breathed deeply, filling her lungs with the cold air. Coming to a stone bench which she used to sit on as a child, she did as she had done then, only this time without her mother. She stared at the shadows the towering trees cast over the lawns, thinking that she should be happy to be back home, where everything was familiar to her and held so many precious memories of her mother. Yet an inexplicable heaviness weighed on her heart.

It didn't help, either, that her thoughts kept returning to that devastating kiss John had given her. His strength and his virility made her feel so very feminine for the first time in her life, his earthy sensuousness so very desirable. Perhaps he hadn't been as affected by that embrace as she had been. He was a soldier, the kind of man who would have known many women on his adventures. In no time at all he would have forgotten about it entirely. Yet she couldn't forget.

Sensing that she wasn't alone, she looked across the lawn and saw the figure of a man coming towards her, his footsteps almost soundless on the thick carpet of grass, then he was directly in front of her. A thrill of excitement tingled along her nerves. How strange that he should appear when she was thinking of him. He had an indefinable brand of swagger and strength and a charming air of mockery and yet admiration in his bold eyes. It was a look that made her heart tremble. He stopped in front her.

'What are you doing out here? I thought you would be abed at this time, that you would be worn out after the journey.'

'I needed to get out of the house for a while.' Getting to her feet, she began to walk slowly along the path, away from the house. John fell into step beside her. 'So much has happened today. I'm tired, but I don't feel like going to bed just yet,' she said softly. 'I'm trying not to think of anything but being back here—at Oakdene—to reminisce. Don't you feel like going to bed either?'

'Not yet. I saw you leave the house so I thought I'd come and keep you company. If you want company, that is.'

Turning her head, she smiled at him. 'I welcome it—providing it isn't Blanche.'

He laughed softly. 'She hasn't changed—still the same. Outspoken and forthright.'

'And extremely vexing. I haven't seen James. She told me not to mention him to my father, which I thought odd. I'm to meet him tomorrow.'

'I am truly sorry for the way she spoke to you at supper. It was totally inappropriate under the circumstances.'

'I expected nothing less from her. She'd already paid me a visit earlier to tell me of the close relationship she'd had with Thomas—not in the least penitent.

My father must have a will of iron to withstand her constant carping.'

'Nevertheless, you do not appear to be unduly disturbed by the closeness that existed between Blanche and Thomas. Most young ladies of my acquaintance would be scandalised by such a relationship.'

Catherine's eyes narrowed and she glanced at him sharply, her cheeks flaming suddenly, for she was stung by the irony and what she considered to be an underlying note of reproof in his voice. For the first time a constraint had come between them. 'Then the young ladies you speak of must be exceedingly dull company, who no doubt spend their time talking of tedious matters like the state of their health and the clothes they wear. I am not like that.'

'It wasn't a reproach, but I am beginning to realise you are quite uninhibited.'

'That is a natural characteristic of mine. Perhaps I should not have silenced Blanche when she was giving such a vivid account of my character, for then I think you would know me a little better.'

'So there is some truth in her description of you,' John remarked, stifling a grin at the complete absence of contrition on her lovely upturned face and jutting chin. 'You are a stubborn and disobedient woman, whose whims must be humoured at all cost.'

Catherine looked at him sharply. 'She never said that.'

'No.' He laughed. 'I thought I'd add my own impression.'

Her unabashed gaze locked on his. 'I see. Then allow me to add a little more and you will learn that some of my pastimes at Carlton Bray were considered by my neighbours to be quite shocking.'

'I would?'

'Yes. I hunt. I fish. I wear breeches like a man— which you already know—and ride about the countryside like a gypsy—which would drive my father to distraction if he knew the full extent of my decadence. I also speak my mind—which you are aware of—for since I had no one to answer to I did not feel that I have to curb my tongue. I do not feel the need to apologise and nor am I ashamed of what I am or what I do, so if this does not meet with your approval, then it is just too bad.'

John cocked a sleek black brow, a merry twinkle of amusement dancing in his eyes. 'I do believe you are trying to shock me, Catherine,' he said calmly. 'But there is nothing about your character that I do not already know.'

'You can read my mind?'

'You might say that. In fact, I am beginning to feel heartily sorry for your father. You appear to be quite a handful.' He chuckled. 'There's little wonder he was eager to marry you off at sixteen.'

Catherine glanced at him. His face was in shadow and he looked at her appreciatively as they strolled slowly along the path. For a moment she forgot her outburst and wondered what it would be like to love and to be loved by such a man as this. His manner was of complete assurance—and a cynical humour twinkled in his eyes. There was also a dangerous, cool reckless-ness about him and a distinct air of adventure.

'Aren't you shocked by my unseemly behaviour, John?' She met his eyes and saw they were teasing and suddenly he laughed outright, a deep, rich sound, and she relaxed.

'Not in the least. It is part of your make-up that I like about you—regardless of what Blanche says.'

'She makes it obvious that she resents my presence here. I shall try my utmost to keep out of her way—which will be difficult, I know, inhabiting the same house. Tomorrow I will spend some time with my fa-ther—if she will permit me to see him alone.'

'You must insist.'

A companionable silence fell between them. Cathe-rine was reassured and comforted by his presence. She shivered slightly as she felt the full force of his mas-culinity, his vigour, the strong pull of his magnetism wrap itself about her. Her rampaging emotions and imaginings where John was concerned were of a per-sonal nature and were beginning to disturb her greatly.

Ever since he had come to Carlton Bray she had tried to ignore them, but they invaded her mind con-stantly, beckoning, like mischievous imps playing a teasing game, flitting to and fro when she was least expecting it. He had established himself firmly in her thoughts and she was becoming painfully aware of him as a man, of his blatant sensuality, and of the excitement that coursed through her with his every glance and each spoken word.

His face was all shadow and planes in the moon's glow. He was so tall, so handsome. She felt a hollow ache inside as he gazed down at her. Reaching the end of the path, she paused and turned to him. She lifted her face and he gently touched her cheek with the backs of his fingers, looking into the liquid depths of her eyes.

'You are incredibly lovely, Catherine. I wonder if you have any idea how lovely you are.'

His voice was soft and melodious. Catherine stood very still, barely able to breathe, yet she was trembling inside. They were so close. She caught her breath, wanting him to draw her into his arms, to breathe in the scent of his flesh, for him to hold her close, to feel the hardness of his body. The warm trickle of a familiar sensation ran through her, a stirring she had felt before when he had kissed her. But they had agreed it wouldn't happen again, that it had been a mistake. His hand curved round her cheek. As she gazed into those fathomless dark eyes, a curious sharp thrill ran through her as the force between them seemed to ignite.

'I know we said we would not repeat what we did at the inn, Catherine, but I suddenly find myself regretting my words. Would you mind if I kissed you again—just to see if it's as wonderful as I remember?'

Unnerved and thoroughly confused at the way things were going, Catherine shook her head. She knew she should refuse, but was so entranced by the moment, by his presence, that she couldn't if she tried. He was smiling, calmly watching her from beneath lowered lids, but Catherine felt he was alert and that unfettered power struggle beneath his calm was about to be unleashed. His tone was perfectly natural, as if he were merely asking her to take a stroll with him, but its very ordinariness caused a feeling of panic and the mystery of the unknown to flow through her. Strands of hair drifted over her face which he drew back and tucked behind her ear. She saw the deepening light in his eyes and the thick, defined brows and wanted to touch him as one touches the soft flesh of a newborn babe.

'We shouldn't,' she whispered her objection, but did not pull back. She was breathing faster as his lips came close and she braced herself for some physical assault.

'We should,' he countered.

Stunned into quiescence, Catherine stood and tilted her head and remained completely still as his lips settled on hers. They were soft and surprisingly cool as they brushed lightly against her closed mouth. A jolt slammed through her as they began to move on hers, thoroughly and possessively exploring every tender contour. With a feeling that this was all wrong, half-stifled, her head reeling, she found herself imprisoned in a grip of steel, pressed against his hard, muscular length, her breasts coming to rest against his chest. There was little she could do to escape and, as her own desire began to stir, she had no wish to.

His lips increased their pressure, becoming coaxing as he slid the tip of his tongue into the warm sweetness of her mouth. She gasped, totally innocent of the sort of warmth, the passion he was skilfully arousing in her, that poured through her veins with a shattering explosion of delight. It was a kiss of exquisite restraint and, unable to think of anything but the exciting urgency of his mouth and the warmth of his breath, she felt herself falling slowly into a dizzying abyss of sensuality. His hands glided restlessly, possessively, up and down her spine and the nape of her neck, pressing her tightly to his hardened body.

Trailing her hands up the muscles of his chest and shoulders and sliding her fingers into the crisp hair at his nape, with a quiet moan of helpless surrender she clung to him, devastated by what he was doing to her, by the raw hunger of his passion. Inside her an emotion began to sweetly unfold, before vibrantly bursting with a fierceness that made her tremble.

John's mouth left her lips and shifted across her cheek to her ear, his tongue flicking and exploring each sensitive crevice, then trailing back to her lips and claiming them once more. His kiss became more demanding, ardent, persuasive, a slow, erotic seduction, tender, wanting, his tongue sliding across her lips, urging them to part. She became lost in a wild and beautiful madness, with blood beating in her throat and temples that wiped out all reason and will. When she moaned softly beneath the sensual onslaught and opened her mouth and kissed him as deeply and erotically as he was kissing her, he groaned with pleasure at the sweetness of her response.

When at last he lifted his mouth from hers, his breathing was harsh and rapid, and gazing up at him Catherine felt as if she would melt beneath his scorching eyes. Slowly she brought one of her hands from behind his neck and her fingers gently traced the outline of his cheek, following the angular line of his jaw and neck.

'Well,' he said, his voice low and husky, recovering more quickly than Catherine. Her face was bemused, her eyes unfocused, her soft pink mouth partly open. 'I think you enjoy being kissed.' When she did not immediately reply, he grinned and murmured, 'Surely I cannot have rendered you speechless.'

'It certainly took my breath, and, yes, I liked it very much,' she confessed, still drifting between total peace and a strange, delirious joy, while at the same time a feeling of disquiet was creeping over her as her mind came together from the regions of the universe where it had fled. Without logic or reason she was drawn to John Stratton as to no other and she experienced a moment of terror when she was with him, for the sheer magnitude of her feelings threatened to overwhelm her. She felt weak, vulnerable, suddenly at his mercy and standing on the threshold of something new. He was essentially worldly, emanating raw power that was an irresistible attraction to any woman. She was stimulated by him, he excited her and he exuded an element of danger that added to the excitement.

But this was not just another adventure and if she entered into any kind of commitment with him then there would be no escape.

Chapter Five

Releasing his hold on her, John gently cradled her chin with his hand. In the pale glow of the moon she was very lovely, with the dreamy, faraway look in her eyes and the passion his kiss had aroused in her softening her features. With the darkness of his eyes glowing with passion still smouldering within their depths, they looked intently into hers.

'You have the body and mind of a clever woman, Lady Stratton, but in worldly experience you are still a child—and I thank God for it.'

'I'm not such a child, John. I have been married, don't forget—and I do know the difference between right and wrong. I should regret what we have just done, rebuke myself, and if you were a gentleman you would forget all about it.'

John let out a long sigh and quietly and without emotion said, 'What you ask is impossible. It happened and neither of us can erase it from our minds. And now

I think you should return to your chamber and go to bed. The hour is late. It's been a long day.'

In a daze of suspended yearning and confusion, Catherine hesitated as his eyes held hers in one long, compelling look, holding all her frustrated longings and unfulfilled desires, everything that was between them there. That one kiss had been too much and too little, arousing deep feelings she did not fully understand. What had happened between them had been a sudden overwhelming passion, heightened by the intensity of the knowledge that it shouldn't be happening.

'Come,' John said, taking her arm. 'I'll walk with you back to the house.'

They walked in silence for a few moments, giving them both time to bring a calmness to their minds.

At length, Catherine said, 'You are close to my father. That is obvious. He speaks well of you.'

'I respect him. He is a grave man, bowed by the troubles and those of the country. And if he has faults—what man has not? It is not for me to judge him.'

Catherine inclined her head and said no more, half envying this certainty and respect for a man who had kept her at arm's length all her life. After a moment, her thoughts turning to Thomas, she said, 'I don't know what I would have done if Thomas had come back. I could not bear the thought of living with him again—being married to him.'

'I know you didn't find marriage to him palatable.

I also know of few well-bred ladies who married for love—but in many cases it comes with marriage.'

'Not in my case. Did you see him before he died?'

'No—I arrived in Newcastle too late.'

'How did he die? Was he ill—wounded?'

'He never fully recovered from a near fatal wound inflicted on him at Marston Moor—and he was wounded again at Preston. I do not believe he had changed—if anything his bitterness that the cause he fought for was lost was worse. War had changed him— as it has so many. Some have nothing left.'

'Neither had Thomas. You must be prepared for what his lawyer will reveal. The truth is that Thomas agreed to marry me for my money. Yes, my father was generous with my dowry and Thomas believed there would be more. But once wed, he found he had no control over my money or the property left to me by my mother, the whole being in the power of trustees who act solely in my interest. When I refused to hand it over to Thomas, he—he used me ill.'

'I'm sorry, Catherine. Why didn't you give it to him? He was your husband. Many would say it was his right.'

'It was not. He married me without love or consideration. I did not hold back out of pity or anger, but because I firmly believed it was the wisest thing to do. Had I not done so he would have poured it into the King's coffers to fund the King's war. I did not want that. I wanted no part in it.'

John stopped and looked down at her. 'Where did

your allegiance lie, Catherine? King or Parliament? I confess to being somewhat bewildered. I realise that being married to a man who bore such a strong allegiance to King Charles it would be both supportive and necessary for a wife to share her husband's beliefs.'

'I told you I am my own woman, John. As a matter of fact, I didn't hold a candle for either side. For me it wasn't about that, it was about survival, about getting through each new day without being fired upon and making sure people were safe, having enough to eat and taken care of. Now it is over I thank God that I kept hold of my mother's legacy, which gives me my independence. I suppose my attitude to the war was somewhat cynical. Living at Carlton Bray, away from everything, I felt somewhat detached. Oh, we had a few skirmishes along the way, but we survived, if somewhat poorer.'

'What you did went way beyond the bounds of courage. You are a very beautiful and desirable young woman. You did well.'

Catherine flushed, unused to such compliments. 'I must have cut a sorry figure when you arrived at Carlton Bray.'

'No. Quite the opposite, in fact,' he said, turning her hands palm upwards, showing no surprise on seeing the startling evidence of the part she had played on helping to keep the castle safe. The soft pads beneath her fingers were marred with a few hard callouses.

Catherine grimaced. 'They are hardly the hands of a well-bred lady.'

'They are beautiful hands—hands to be proud of,' he murmured, bending his head and kissing them softly, taking her completely by surprise. 'Never be ashamed of your hands, Catherine.'

Only when he raised his head and released his hold on her hands did she step back, her cheeks flushed in bewilderment so that she did not know what to think.

John stayed where he was, smiling slowly as he watched her walk back to the house, knowing that his kiss had stirred an unknown part of her untouched by Thomas. Yes, it had stirred an unknown passion in her innocent heart. She was like a fragile flower, fragrant and sweet, and as ignorant of just how tantalising and sensual she was.

Catherine returned to her room, her mind in a whirl. John had awoken in her a need otherwise unknown to her, one she did not understand. She had struggled and fought invading forces over the years, enduring without complaint all the indignities, sufferings and hardships they imposed, but it had taken just one kiss from John Stratton to break down every barrier of her carefully held reserve. She was so preoccupied with her thoughts that she thought she was imagining it when she heard the sudden cry of a child. She paused to listen. The cry came once more, fainter now, as if the child was being comforted. Realising that it must be James, she gave it no more thought and went to bed.

She lay sleepless, physically exhausted yet unable to still the confusion of thoughts in her head or quell the tempest of her emotions. The house was silent, but the noises of the sleeping countryside came to her through the half-open window—the shriek of an owl and the bark of a fox sounded somewhere deep in the woods.

She had tossed and turned until, in the early hours, she heard the crying again. Getting out of bed, she crossed to the door and listened. The child was still crying and seemed to be quite distressed. Shoving her feet into her slippers, she threw her robe about her shoulders.

Moving silently along the landing, she climbed the stairs to the second floor where she paused, straining her eyes in the dark. The house was just as ghostly at night as she remembered. The floorboards creaked and the clock in the hall ticked ponderously. A light showed beneath the nursery door. Taking a deep breath, she pushed it open.

The unfamiliar scene in the candlelit room made her stop short and catch her breath. The sight of a maid she did not recognise seated before the fire with a young boy on her lap, cradling him while his sobs turned to gulps, touched her heart. She was clearly failing in her task to quieten him. Sensing her presence, the maid turned her head, startled when she saw her. Catherine stepped inside and closed the door.

'What have we here?' she asked. When the maid would have got up she held out her hand. Catherine noted how tired she looked, her young face strained with anxiety. 'No—please don't get up. I heard the child crying, so I came to see.' Looking down at the boy, she smiled, crouching down so that she was on a level with him. A pair of dark eyes were looking back at her. He was a handsome boy with curly nut-brown hair. 'Hello,' she said softly. 'You must be James.'

'Yes,' the maid confirmed when the child hiccupped and, overcome with shyness, buried his face in the maid's shoulder, shoving two fat little fingers in his mouth.

'And is he not well? Is that why he's crying? He looks flushed.'

'I think he has a tooth coming through. The mistress told me to wake her if he was poorly.'

'The mistress?'

'His mother.'

'Then—then I think you should go and get her. I'll stay with James if you like.'

'Oh—thank you, only—well—he clings to me and...'

Seeing how firmly the child was holding on to the maid, Catherine stood up. 'Don't worry. Stay here with James. I'll go and fetch her.'

With her thoughts running riot inside her head Catherine knocked softly on Blanche's door, waiting for it to be opened. Having been woken from sleep, attired in a flowing nightdress and with her hair unbound, Blanche eventually opened the door. She looked surprised to find Catherine standing there.

'Catherine! It's late. What is it you want?'

'Your son is crying, Blanche. According to his nurse he wants his mother.'

Without a word Blanche went and got her robe, wrapping it about her. 'I'll go and see him.'

'Your son, Blanche. I have a brother—a half-brother.' Catherine fixed Blanche with a hard stare. 'Why did no one write to inform me?'

'If you really want to know, then ask your father. He will tell you. Now you must excuse me. I must tend to James or he'll keep us all awake with his crying.'

Following a night with little sleep, the morning found Catherine bolstering her nerve to enter her father's room. The curtains were pulled halfway across the window—apparently he didn't like too much light—and a vast canopied bed dominated the room. She had prepared herself to take him to task over the child. Fortunately Blanche was occupied elsewhere. He was in bed. The maid had taken away his breakfast tray, the food only pecked at. Catherine went to the bed and looked down at him.

'How are you feeling this morning, Father?'

'Tired. I sleep all night and still I'm tired.' He glanced at her. 'You have seen him?'

'Who?'

'The boy.'

'Yes, I have. Last night. I heard a child crying and went to the old nursery to see him. He's a delightful child. Why was I not told I have a brother? Why was it kept from me?'

'Because he is not my son—and has nothing to do with you. I do not want him near me. I have no plans to let him inherit anything of mine.'

Catherine stared at him, astounded. 'Not your son? But—then who…?'

Edward's eyes were so sharp that they almost penetrated her skull. 'Do I need to tell *you* that—you of all people?'

Catherine turned away, her hands balled into fists hidden in the folds of her skirt. 'Thomas,' she uttered. 'He is Thomas's son?' She turned back to her father, her face hard. 'But how can that be, when Thomas went missing after Marston Moor?'

'Use your head, girl. Nothing was heard of him when the Royalists were routed back in forty-four. Nothing was heard of him because he was holed up in York at Murton House, hardly a stone's throw from Marston Moor. Do you forget that Blanche is from York? She was there with her parents at that time. 'Tis not a coincidence he found himself beneath her roof. He had wounds from the battle, but still he managed to find his way to her. She was there with him. She had him secreted away for six months before he fled over the border to collude with the Scots and she came back to Oakdene.'

'But her parents…'

'Are old. And her father was knocked on the head at Naseby and he's been mad ever since. His wife is no better. They wouldn't have batted an eyelid if the King himself had taken up residence at Murton House.

That boy isn't mine—however determined Blanche is to make everyone believe it—but I know the truth.'

'I'm sorry, Father. I know how much you wanted a son.'

'Aye—well… I want her out of this house. Her and that boy. When I am gone not one penny will go her way. I want you to see to it.'

'But—she is your wife and entitled to—'

'She is entitled to nothing,' he flared, his face becoming flushed with the exertion. His hands tightened on the bedclothes. 'I have every right to do as I think fit. She lied, deceived and cheated on me—with my own son-in-law. Your husband.' He eyed her steadily. 'You know, don't you, that she and Thomas were lovers?'

'No—although I always suspected it. Blanche confirmed my suspicion when I arrived yesterday.'

'The woman is shameless. I cannot forgive her—nor can I accept the boy as mine, which is what she wants. My body is weak, but my mind is as sharp as it has always been and I will not be made a fool of. How can he be mine when I wasn't around at his conception? She has pushed my tolerance beyond all bearing with her faithlessness and her duplicity. She'll get nothing from me for that boy.'

His anger brought on a fit of coughing that left him weak when it subsided. Catherine helped him to some water before sitting on the bed and facing him.

'Try not to upset yourself. It will weaken you more.'

He looked at her with more understanding than she

had given him credit for and when he next spoke his voice was soft. 'I know that I have a good advocate in you and it is an onerous task I have set you. You are my best hope to see that my wishes are carried out when I'm gone. Will you do that?'

Catherine nodded. 'Yes,' she answered quietly. 'I promise you that I will do my very best.'

'That is all I ask. I have never met a woman more capable of carrying out the responsibility. Pity you weren't born a boy. You've shown more mettle than most men I know. You've not had a happy time of it, have you, Catherine?'

'No. Far from it.' Looking back on those six years she had been married to Thomas, she saw them as dark, miserable years, blackened by disappointment and humiliation, with no gaiety, no companionship.

'I am sorry that it had to be like this,' he said, his voice no more than a hoarse whisper. 'I haven't long left on this earth. I know that. One of my greatest sorrows is that I married you to Thomas—but he got what he deserved in the end,' he said softly. 'I speak sincerely when I say that my intention of bringing you here was to make amends for what I did—what I put you through.'

Looking into her father's eyes, Catherine saw that he spoke the truth. For the first time in her life she took his frail hand from the coverlet.

'You will stay with me, will you, until...?'

Catherine nodded and smiled. 'I'm not going anywhere, Father. Now get some rest.'

* * *

Catherine waited until her father slept and then she left him, more angry, confused and emotional than she had ever been. What had he meant when he said that Thomas had got what he deserved? Was there something being kept from her? For the first time in many years she gave way to scalding tears. They ran unheeded down her cheeks. Never had she felt so worthless, so unimportant, so neglected, so humiliated. After a moment she dashed her tears away. With all this going round in her head she refused to be looked on as a victim, but… Oh, God, how it hurt.

Going outside with the intention of putting as much distance as she possibly could from the house and its inhabitants, she encountered John having just stabled his horse after his visit to Windsor Castle. Her hair was dishevelled and tears coursed their way down her cheeks. He was the last person she wanted to see just then.

John stared at her in alarm, falling in step beside her as she walked. Not until they had traversed the gardens and entered the trees beyond did he take her arm and bring her to a halt. 'Catherine? For heaven's sake, tell me what is wrong—what has happened to upset you so?'

'Did you know? Did you know that James is Thomas's son and not my father's—that he bears no relationship to me whatsoever?' She glanced about, unable to settle her misting gaze on a single object while her mind went round in circles.

John reached out and took her arm, turning her to face him. 'Catherine—don't do this. Don't torture yourself.'

She raised her tear-filled eyes to his. 'Torture? Yes, I've tortured myself for the past six years—but this—this is something I never envisaged—that Blanche would bear him a child.'

'Believe me when I tell you that I did not know James was Thomas's son. Your father never spoke of it and I had no reason to suspect. I'm sorry you had to find out like this.'

'He's such a lovely little boy—he really is adorable. How I wish my father had sired him—that he really was my half-brother. How much more is being kept from me?'

'Your father told you about James—what more is there?'

'I don't know, but there is more—I feel it.' She swept away the wetness from her cheeks, annoyed with herself for showing such weakness. Analysing her feelings, she was desperately hurt. But she was honest enough to admit to herself that it was mainly her pride that had been wounded. 'All the time my husband was in York being entertained by Blanche, there was I, not knowing if I was still a wife or a widow. Oh, how I wish I'd never come to Oakdene. I should have gone to Wilsden instead.'

John looked her over with a brazen stare and cocked a dubious brow. 'What? And deprived me of the pleasure of your company?' He chuckled. 'Shame on you,

Catherine Stratton,' he teased softly. 'Spare a thought for the disappointment I would have felt had you done so. Besides, you had to come to London to see Thomas's lawyer about the will.'

'Not necessarily. I would have made him come to me,' she replied, somewhat petulantly. Tilting her head, she looked at him quizzically. 'Did you really enjoy my company? Did it not occur to you that I might be behaving like a trollop when I let you kiss me?'

'I never thought you were anything other than what you are. I wanted to kiss you and, had you been devoted to Thomas and genuinely grieving his loss, then I would not have done that. I should have known what would happen when I agreed to let you ride to London with me. You're not a woman a man can ignore. I want you, Catherine. I've had many women—I cannot deny that, or that I enjoyed each one—but none of them meant anything to me. I was constantly involved in war. They were a diversion. Would that you were a diversion, too. So don't cheapen what we did. Yes, you are Thomas's widow. But when were you ever a wife?'

The words hung in the air between them. Catherine stared at him, unable to contradict his statement, for she knew he spoke the truth. The warmly mellow tones of his voice were imbued with a rich quality that seemed to vibrate through her womanly being. To her amazement, the sound evoked a strangely pleasurable disturbance in areas far too private for her to consider just them. As evocative as the sensations were, she didn't quite know what to make of them. All she was conscious of just then was a sense of complication and confusion. Everything had suddenly changed. John's powerful, animal-like masculinity was an assault on her senses. Moistening her lips, she could almost feel her body offer itself to this man and, in that instant, both acknowledged the flame that ignited between them.

'I was not aware of your situation, Catherine. I had no contact with Thomas after Marston Moor. At that time I was dealing with my own loss—my father and my elder brother. With my two younger brothers taking care of their families, I had to ensure that my mother and sister were safe and to offer them what comfort I could.'

Catherine was suddenly mortified. Compassion swelled in her heart as she realised that although he always appeared in control and unemotional, John's loss was great indeed. She had lost her husband, but she did not mourn him.

'Of course you were,' she said, her expression one of regret. 'How thoughtless of me. You told me—I should have known better. I am sorry for your tragic loss. It must have been hard for you—especially for your mother.'

'Yes, it was—it is. It's not something one gets over easily—if ever.'

'No, is isn't. I was close to my mother. She died nine years ago. I still feel her loss, but my memories of her help.'

'Happy ones?'

'Oh, yes.'

'There wasn't a family in England that didn't lose a loved one at some time or other during the wars. Whatever the truth of the matter, your father should have informed you about James.'

'Blanche has tried forcing him to accept James as his—but he knows the truth and he is determined to cast them both out without a penny. I've never been close to my father—in fact, there have been times when what I felt has been as close to hate as it could possibly be. But what Blanche has done to him is cruel. She should be exposed for what she has done.'

'And who do you think will benefit from that? Think what it will mean. Your father will suffer the shame of his wife's adultery with his son-in-law. The story will become common gossip. For his sake and your own—not forgetting the child whom it will affect most of all in the future—you must say nothing.'

She stared at him, uncomprehending. 'My sake?'

'Thomas was your husband. It was bad enough that he had an affair with your stepmother, but there is a child as a result of their union and he must be taken into consideration.'

She cast him a mutinous look. 'They should be punished for what they have done.'

'It's not as if you can punish Thomas. As for Blanche…'

'What she has done to me and my father is wicked.'

'Nothing in life is quite so simple—or fair,' John said gently, tucking a rebellious lock of her hair behind her ear. 'Thomas was a man like any other and every man suffers from periodic moments of desire when they are with a beautiful woman.'

'Even you?'

'Even me—which is what happened between us. We are all human, Catherine.

'I think I hate Thomas.'

'But Edward is your father. His health must be taken into consideration. For his sake you must harness your emotions and remain strong.'

'My plans were to go directly to Wilsden, but my father has asked me to remain at Oakdene until such a time as he dies.'

'Then that is what you must do. Afterwards, when he is deceased, you can decide what to do about Blanche—although he must set it down in his will. He must send for his lawyer if he wishes to make any changes. It will be complicated, whatever is decided. But try not to be too hard on Blanche. It has not been easy for her either—far from it, in fact. And she cares for James deeply. She is a loving mother and very protective of him,'

Catherine continued to look at John for a long moment. Only gradually did she come to accept that bringing the incident out into the open would subject her father to unnecessary pain while resolving nothing.

'Will you walk with me?'

Catherine shook her head. 'No. I'm poor company just now. So much has happened that I have much to think about. I think I should return to my father.'

John stepped back. 'As you wish. Tomorrow I have arranged to see Thomas's lawyer. We'll set off at about ten o'clock and ride into the city.'

'Yes. I'll be ready.'

Choked by a terrible miasma of loneliness and deprivation—feelings she recognised having grown up with them—Catherine shut herself in her chamber, hoping that no one would intrude. When she had come to Oakdene, she had been buoyed up with expectancy, but now, in the light of what she had discovered in the last twenty-four hours, her future was bleak, as were her prospects. With her mind on the child and how painful his presence at Oakdene must be for her father, she became unnaturally calm, as calm as a block of ice that has no warmth.

Later, having eaten her evening meal with her father in his room, she retired to her chamber, intending to go to bed. Looking out of the window and seeing it had started to snow, she perched on the window seat and watched it fall against the darkness of the night. Her thoughts turned to John. She tried to think of him dispassionately, not to let her emotions become involved, because if she did she was in danger of being overwhelmed by him. He had a way of intruding into her thoughts when her desire was to keep him out.

He was different to any man she had ever met and he had made a deep impression on her. Never had she met a man who was so alive, so full of confidence, a man who both stimulated and excited her. He had a sensuous way of regarding her that made her physically aware of herself as a woman.

With these thoughts occupying her mind, she breathed deeply and let her eyes follow the gently falling snowflakes. She was about to get up when her attention became riveted on a man who appeared out of the darkness of the trees and paused to look at the snow-draped garden. It was John and he was about to walk towards the house but, as if sensing her watching him, he tilted his head and looked up at her window.

Without moving her position, she gazed down into his upturned face, feeling a searing stab of raw emotion pierce her heart. She remembered how it had felt when he held her, the caress of his finger when he had drawn it gently down her cheek. Holding his gaze, she saw there was something in his eyes that made her heart beat wildly—a softness, a glow. What was the meaning of it? What was the magic of the man when once again, with just a look, he could make her feel the melting sensation in her secret parts? His gaze was like a potent caress as she looked down into his brooding dark eyes.

Raising his hand, with an enigmatic smile and small wave he turned and entered the house. She was tempted to go down to receive him, but, realising the danger of doing so at this hour, she climbed into bed. Sleep eluded her as she tossed and turned until the early hours of the morning because of him, then her dreams were filled with such longings and yearnings as she never thought to experience.

The following day was cold, but thankfully fine for their ride into the city and Lincoln's Inn. The snow had melted with the dawn. Catherine questioned the use of horses in favour of the coach, but John pointed out that once they entered the city they would make better progress on horseback. Shrouded in long cloaks, their hair concealed beneath tall hats, they rode in silence. Catherine couldn't resist sneaking a glance at her companion. The sight of him on the spirited stallion with its high-flying tail drew her admiration. Horse and rider flowed along together.

The sun's rays trailed across the unfolding landscape and a silvery mist hung over the London skyline on the horizon, its church spires and parapets providing a jagged edge. On reaching the outskirts, Catherine was both enthralled and repelled in equal measure. It was six years since she had been there and it was exactly as she remembered. It seethed with noisy activity beneath a noxious cloud of smoking chimneys and gutters running down the streets, choked with all manner of refuse. Animals, carriages and hand-drawn barrows all vied for right of way. Beggars and starving children rummaged for food while the prosperous openly despised them for their suffering.

'The poor are always with you,' John said on seeing Catherine's appalled and distressed expression.

'So it would seem,' she replied, wondering if it

would ever return to how it had been before the war, with music and dancing and the theatres and the King's scandal-ridden court. Not that she had experienced any of it herself, but she had loved listening to the gossip the servants brought with them to Oakdene. She was relieved when they entered a better part of town, with smart streets and houses with Palladian façades inhabited by the rich.

On locating the address of Mr Isaac Morton, they were expected and shown into his office. Mr Morton, Thomas's lawyer, was to preside over the legal affairs. His offices used to be in Worcester until he upped and settled in London. John took him aside and spoke quietly to him on what he told Catherine was a private matter before proceedings began.

After expressing sympathy for their loss, seated at a large, highly polished desk and surrounded by books and papers, with his elderly grey head bowed over Thomas Stratton's last will and testament, he quickly got down to business. After he had read out the small gifts Thomas had bequeathed to his loyal retainers, who would be notified shortly, he focused his gaze on the two remaining recipients.

'What I am about to disclose will not come as anything surprising and you will understand that with the country at war the will was written at a very difficult time. The estate has suffered somewhat—which has been the case in many landed families throughout England. Unfortunately, Lord Stratton beggared himself when he poured the majority of his wealth into the

King's coffers. It's an expensive business, raising a troop of horse and financing their needs for an indefinite period. The expense and the necessary work to put it right has brought you extra responsibility, I'm afraid.'

'And nothing at the end of it, it would seem,' Catherine commented bitterly.

'I am sorry, Lady Stratton, but that's how it is. There are no other dependents other than those I have named. There is the inheritance and resources you brought to the marriage, Lady Stratton. In normal times you would have equal jointure from the estate, but these are not normal times. You also keep the property of Wilsden Manor in the town of Hereford, which was in your own inheritance from your mother and, as I understand it, is being managed by her trustees.'

'It is as I expected,' Catherine said. 'I am aware of the terms of the settlement that were negotiated and agreed upon with my father and Thomas on our betrothal.'

'The whole of the property—that is, the land, Carlton Bray Castle, and other properties—since the demise of your father and elder brother are to go to you, sir, as his direct heir of the Sussex line of Strattons. I trust this is in accordance with what you were expecting.'

'It is,' John said, 'although living life on the Welsh Marches is not the life I had planned.'

'You are to leave the army, I believe.'

John nodded. 'Yes. I am done with fighting. I hope

to leave London for my family home in Sussex within the next week.'

'Just in time for Christmas. Let us hope that the last foray at Preston will be the end of it and you can enjoy your retirement. However,' he said, looking up from the document and peering at them both anxiously, 'there is something else. I told you at the beginning that this will was written at the beginning of the war. Since then Lord Stratton added a codicil, just days before his death. I received word from him from Newcastle where he had been imprisoned for several weeks. He was also suffering from severe wounds he acquired at the battle at Preston in August this year. He was a much valued client, so I took ship for Newcastle as soon as I received the letter.'

John cast him a puzzled look. 'I knew nothing about a codicil.'

'He must have had his reasons.'

'Does it pose a problem? Does it alter the inheritance?' asked Catherine, wary of what was to come.

'No, but—it is a delicate matter, my lady. However, it might be of some comfort to you knowing you were in his thoughts at the very end and that he had your best interest—and those of the estate—at heart.'

Catherine stared at him in disbelief. In fact, she would have laughed were the situation not of so serious a nature. 'Pardon me if I appear surprised, Mr Morton, but my husband was not known to be sentimental. To my knowledge he never considered anyone other than himself.' Her words were critical and condemning, but she would not believe that Thomas's thoughts had been favourable to her at the very end.

'No—well, he made it clear to me that he was concerned that you, being a young woman, possibly taking up residence at Wilsden Manor on his demise, would be unprotected should the war continue and that you would be more secure if you were to return to your father's house, Oakdene House, in London.'

Catherine shook her head in bewilderment. 'But—what has that to do with a codicil? There has to be more.'

Mr Morton coughed nervously. 'Yes—there is. It concerns your stepmother—Blanche Kingsley.'

A cold hand clutched at Catherine's heart. 'Blanche? But—I don't understand…'

'He—your husband—discovered he had a son—born to Blanche Kingsley three years ago.'

Silence followed his pronouncement, the words hanging in the air of the small office.

'I'm sorry, Lady Stratton. This must be painful for you to hear.'

'It doesn't matter,' Catherine replied, almost choking on the words. 'I am already aware of my late husband's indiscretion. Pray continue, Mr Morton. I want to know everything.'

'Very well. It was important to him that the child would be taken care of. As in illegitimate child he could not inherit the estate or title. Lord Stratton's wealth was gone and Carlton Bray would be sequestered. Knowing this and that the title and estate would pass to you, sir,' Mr Morton said, directing his gaze at John once more, 'because you are his heir and a Parliament man, he took comfort in the knowledge that the estate would remain in the Stratton family.'

John nodded. 'I expect that to be the case.'

'Lord Stratton recommends that should the war break out once more, you might look to the preservation of Carlton Bray Castle any way you can.'

'That won't happen,' John stated, confident in his experience and knowledge of the present state of the nation. 'The Royalists are finished.'

'He was confident that you would look at the facts and decide what is to be done for the best. However, he realised that he had no right to put pressure on you, no right at all. He states that despite the differences that divided you during the war, he knows you to be an honourable man and that family is important to you. Knowing Blanche has no means of her own to support herself and his son and that Sir Edward would exclude her from his will because of their adulterous affair, he asks that you see she and his son James are comfortably housed and that you see to his education.'

His expression closed, John nodded. 'My cousin has given me much to consider. I will, of course, think over what is to be done that will benefit all concerned. However, we must not forget that Sir Edward is still very much alive and, while ever Blanche and her son have a roof over their heads, nothing can be decided.'

Catherine was sitting perched on the edge of her seat as if her backbone was made of hard steel, her expression unreadable. 'You are right to say that nothing can be decided while ever my father has breath in his body.' She got to her feet, clenching her fists in the folds of her skirts to stop them from shaking. 'Is there anything else, Mr Morton?'

'No, I think that is it, Lady Stratton.'

'I thank you for your time and your patience, Mr Morton. There is just one more thing that I hope you can tell me.'

'Of course. Anything.'

'Who was it who told Thomas he had a son?'

'I believe it to be Sir Edward Kingsley—your father, Lady Stratton.'

'I see. Please excuse me,' she said, turning and crossing to the door with a quiet dignity, having no wish to stay and hear more, only a strong desire to be by herself.

Chapter Six

Not until they were in the street did either of them speak. Thomas's death had affected John deeply, more so since he had inherited Carlton Bray. He would blame himself for ever for arriving too late in Newcastle to speak for his cousin. Because of the opposing forces and heated tempers raging against the Royalists at the time, he had kept his thoughts and feelings to himself, while his heart swelled with hatred against the pitiless fate which had forced degradation on all Strattons.

'It is very much as I expected,' John said, thrusting his hands into his gloves, giving Catherine no notion of his troubled thoughts. 'Do you not agree, Catherine?'

Having recovered some of her self-possession, Catherine drew back her shoulders and lifted her head, the action meaning to tell him she was in control of herself. 'Yes, it was—although I find it hard to accept what Thomas has asked of you. Why would he do that, unless it was for some malicious reason of his own?'

John shot her an angry look. 'Thomas was not insane and nor was he a malicious man.'

Catherine's look was one of scorn. 'Please do not try to defend my husband to me and do not preach to me of his attributes—not that he had any that I saw. Next you will be telling me that I do him a grave injustice, that he was a man of honour and integrity, a man who considered the well-being of others before his own throughout his life. I am sure he thought this over very carefully before adding the codicil. You would be a fool to even consider what he's asked of you.'

'Nevertheless, that is what I will do. When anything happens to your father, Blanche and James's future must be considered.'

'I am sure Blanche will be gratified,' she said coldly. 'Will you tell her about the codicil?'

'No. Least said the better at this time. Plenty of time for that later. As for Carlton Bray—I will take care of matters there—unless, of course, you have become so attached to the place you would like to go back.'

'It was my home for six long years. Despite the troubles I looked on it as my home. But when I left I vowed never to return. I will not go back there. As far as I am concerned, Carlton Bray is the last thing on my mind at this moment. After my miserable marriage to Thomas I want to put it behind me.'

'And you will not be persuaded to marry again in a hurry.' He grinned suddenly. 'Then you are fortunate that Thomas's codicil didn't suggest that I should marry his widow.'

She glowered at him. 'Please don't jest, John, I am not in the mood. I am hardly likely to walk blindly into another marriage—to put myself and my trust completely in another man's power for the whole of my life.'

The smile that broke across John's white teeth Catherine found infuriating. 'Calm your anger, Catherine. This other man you speak of has not asked you to be his wife. I have never forced myself on a woman who didn't want me—and I feel no temptation to do so now. Despite your abrasive manner and waspish tongue, I have seen in your eyes and felt on your lips that which gives me hope for better things.'

Temper flared in Catherine's eyes as hot, angry words bubbled to her lips. 'Then you were mistaken and I will make it plain here and now that I have no intention of changing—and if I do not meet with your expectations then you can go to the devil and be damned. Now, where are our horses? I would like to return to Oakdene. The city is such a dismal place on days such as this.'

The following two days John spent at the army headquarters at Windsor. He was impatient to retire from his military duties so he could go to his home in Sussex, but every day there were fresh tasks to undertake and it was expected at any day that the King would be brought back to London.

He had not seen Catherine since they had returned from London. He was surprised that, hardened soldier though he was, he was unable to cast her from his mind. With a warmth flooding and throbbing through his veins, he remembered how it had felt to hold her, how soft and yielding her lips had been when she had kissed him with such tender passion and how her body had moulded itself innocently into his own. Constantly he found himself dwelling on her warm femininity.

Oakdene was quiet when John returned from Windsor. He looked in the downstairs rooms, but there was no sign of Catherine. A clattering of crockery came from the kitchen. After asking one of the servants to have hot water brought up to his chamber, he went upstairs. Just about to enter his room, he paused in the open doorway when Blanche approached carrying some linen. Her blue gown, which provocatively outlined her contours, was cut revealingly low and the upper part of her breasts enticingly displayed. Her hair was arranged to fall sensually over her shoulders. Unable to ignore her, John smiled. The smile encouraged her for she came to stand close.

'Some hot water is being brought up for you, John. I've brought some clean linen.' Brushing past him, she swept inside his chamber, placing the linen on the end of the bed.

This was the first time he had been entirely alone with her. No man could not be moved by Blanche's beauty. She really was all temptation for any man, but there was only one woman who could tempt John and he was impatient to see her.

'Is there anything else you need? Anything I can get for you?'

'I have everything I need, Blanche. Thank you. How is Edward?'

'Sleeping—he spends most of his days sleeping. He's having his meal in his room later—not that he has an appetite these days.'

Her use of the word appetite was open to two interpretations, one of which was risqué and, he thought, intended. John chose to ignore it and stepped away. As he did so he caught the gleam in her eyes, a gleam that belied the feminine allure. It was not attraction he saw in those narrowed depths, but cold-hearted calculation, and it acted like a bucket of cold water being poured over him. Every muscle tensed. He walked to the door. 'Excuse me, Blanche. The servants will be up with the water for my bath any minute.'

Not to be got rid of so easily, she slowly moved towards him. 'You know, John, Edward is so glad you are here. He's come to rely on you over the years. You have seen how ill he is.'

'In which case it must be a relief to him to have Catherine here. She will be a comfort to him, I am sure.'

Blanche did not want to hear about Catherine. Hearing the door open and close downstairs followed by light footfalls on the stairs, she continued to walk towards him, tripping on the edge of a carpet—intentionally, John was convinced. When she fell forward and it looked as if she might land on the floor, he immediately reached out to save her. When he would have steadied her she fell into his arms. Raising his eyes, he saw Catherine standing in the doorway. He was incredulous, then felt a surge of anger. For mischievous reasons of her own, Blanche's staged trip to fall into his arms so that Catherine would see had been well-timed. Making no attempt to disengage herself, Blanche turned her head, then, feigning a look of surprise, she stepped back.

'Catherine—my goodness! What must you think?'

'Excuse me. I don't think anything. Perhaps the next time you wish to be alone with John you should close the door.'

Blanche's voice was sweet and mock-apologetic as she said, 'Forgive me, Catherine. I never heard you. Must you creep about?'

'I don't creep, Blanche,' she retorted with all the condescension she could muster. However, she merely smiled at John—who had been rendered speechless—and lifted her eyebrows in mockery before she turned her back on them both and carried on to her own chamber.

Thankfully the servants chose that moment to arrive with the hot water. With a soft laugh and telling him to enjoy his bath, having achieved her aim, Blanche left.

Catherine was angry and hurt by what she had just witnessed. She was certain that Blanche was taunting her, but Catherine was determined not to let her get under her skin and arouse her to an expression of her personal feelings. She strongly suspected that the situation had been manipulated by Blanche and that John was too much of a gentleman to defend himself at Blanche's expense.

The house was quiet when Catherine went to sit with her father the next afternoon. He like to have her read to him, even though he always fell asleep halfway into the story. She was surprised to find John seated by the bed, the two men in quiet conversation. They seemed comfortable together. John rose when she entered and crossed to the door.

'Please don't leave on my account,' she said, stepping back on to the landing. 'I was passing and thought Father might like some company. I can come back later.'

'I was about to leave,' he said, pulling the door to behind him before she had time to step away. 'I have things to do. You look pale,' he said softly, keeping his eyes on Catherine with uncomfortable steadiness.

'Am I? I wasn't aware of it,' Catherine replied, trying to hold on to her composure, pretending that she couldn't feel John's eyes on her, querying, trying to probe, gently. As their eyes met his dark brows lifted in bland enquiry. Catherine caught her breath and felt heat scorch through her body before hastily looking away, ashamed that his look made her legs weaken and her heart to race, as it had on that other occasion when he had kissed her so devastatingly and sent her young, innocent heart soaring heavenwards.

'Catherine—about yesterday when you—'

'Please don't think you have to explain anything to me, John.' The last thing she wanted was to give him the satisfaction of knowing it troubled her.

'Nevertheless, I would like to. Blanche had brought some linen to my chamber. She tripped and would have fallen had I not been there to prevent it.'

'How convenient—for her as well as you,' she quipped, unable to help herself.

'Believe me, Catherine, Blanche is a friend and nothing more.'

Knowing he spoke the truth, she began to relax for the first time since they had returned from London. 'Of course she is and I'm sorry if I sounded churlish.' She gave him a teasing smile, mischief dancing in her eyes. 'Although I can't say that I blame her for fluttering her eyelashes in your direction. You are a handsome man, John. I think Blanche sees the day when she will be a widow and has decided to up her status in life. An earl would satisfy her very well. Have a care. She is already sharpening her talons.'

'Blanche is not my type.'

'And what is your type?' she asked. 'You must be very hard to please.'

'I am.' He shook his head slowly, chuckling softly. 'Believe me when I say your suspicions are totally unfounded. There is only one lady in this house that interests me.'

'Is that so? Well, John, I insist that you introduce me

to her one day. There must be someone in the house who has escaped my attention.'

'I will make a point of it. Edward has told me it is a relief that you are here. I entertain him with the latest gossip from Windsor and news of the King. How is it to be home—with your father?'

'It has not been the perfect reconciliation, but I believe we understand each other.'

'I'm glad to hear it.'

'It's strange to see him so helpless. I always thought he was invincible.'

'No one is invincible, Catherine.' Raising his hand, he touched her cheek. 'You look tired. Are you sleeping well?'

'Yes, thank you, John. I sleep very well.'

'I imagine you're missing the clean air of the Welsh Marches. When did you last ride out?'

'When we rode into London.'

'Then tomorrow I will ride with you again—if that suits. It will do you good to have a change of scene.'

Her heart lifted a little at his suggestion. 'Yes— it would. It's a pity it isn't summertime. When I was little my mother would take me to the river,' she said, thinking wistfully of those past days. 'We would take a picnic and walk by the water.'

'Then that is what we will do—although I think the river is rather ambitious. We shall have a picnic of our very own.'

'What? In the middle of winter? Where is the pleasure in that? It would be quite impossible.'

'Whenever I hear that word I am always challenged to disprove it.'

Catherine laughed at him. 'It's far too cold to sit about eating outdoors. Far better to be inside in front of a cosy fire.'

He scowled at her in mock reproof. 'I would never take you for a fair-weather woman, Catherine. I have appreciated many a meal out in the open surrounded by my fellow soldiers—whatever the weather. I can highly recommend it.'

'Very well, John, you have persuaded me. I will arrange it with Mrs Coleman for tomorrow. Now go away while I sit with Father. He'll wonder what we're talking about.'

'Wait,' he said, as she was about to push the door open. 'Have you told him that you know he was the one who told Thomas that he has a son?'

She shook her head. 'No. After much thought I think the matter is best left. He is very ill. There's nothing to be gained by upsetting him.'

'Yes—I agree. Nothing can be done about it now.'

After saying his farewells to Edward, John left them to return to Windsor. Catherine sat in the chair he had occupied beside the bed.

'I'm happy to see you getting on with John.'

'Yes. He's been very kind. You've known him a long time, I believe.'

He nodded. 'I met John through his father, Charles Stratton, at the beginning of the conflict. Charles was influential in my decision to support Parliament.'

'John told me how you were wounded at Edgehill. Why wasn't I informed?'

'It was nothing. I didn't want a fuss. John is a fine man—none finer. He's made of different stuff to his cousin Thomas. I got to know him well and at each battle I marvelled at the speed and decision with which he went into action. Whenever he came to the army headquarters at Windsor and I was at home, he would always make a point of coming to see me. We spent many an hour in conversation—and he plays a mean game of chess.' He turned his head to her, studying her closely for a moment. 'You should seriously think of marrying again, Catherine. You are too young to remain a widow for the rest of your life.'

'I'm in no immediate hurry to wed. I sincerely hope you are not about to suggest someone you consider suitable.'

'No,' he replied after a moment. 'I'd not force you— only suggest—advise—whatever you care to call it. You're a grown woman, a widow. You must decide these matters for yourself.'

The following day was cold with a light covering of snow, but the bright sunshine was an encouragement to leave the house. John, who had spent the night at Windsor, arrived mid-morning. Catherine was dressed in her serviceable breeches beneath her cloak and her hair was fastened back beneath her hat. She pulled on her kid gloves and, with her crop tucked beneath her arm, gave the hamper of food to John to carry. Together they went to the stables, which were relatively quiet apart from a couple of grooms going about their chores.

'I would have asked for one of the horses to be saddled in readiness,' she said, 'but I didn't know what time you would arrive.'

'We'll soon have you saddled up and be on our way.'

'As you see,' Catherine said, walking down the length of stalls, 'there are few horses left to choose from. Before the war, horses, after politics, were my father's abiding passion. Possessing some prime horseflesh, he was immensely proud of his large stable, which was envied and praised by many hereabouts. He loved to hunt and he adored his gun dogs and falcons almost as much as his horses.' Stopping in front of one of the stalls, she opened the door where a brown mare was munching hay from a trough. 'This is Lady. I would have selected the horse I rode into London, but she became lame when one of the boys was exercising her yesterday. Lady should do nicely. She's not been ridden lately so she's in need of some exercise.'

John entered, patting her. The mare responded by arching her neck and whickering softly. 'I'll take a look at her before we set off,' he said, heading off to the tack room.

Catherine stood and calmly watched him prepare to saddle Lady. Before doing so he stood back and looked at her from every angle, picking up a hoof and going on to examine her teeth with a thoroughness that did not surprise her. She sensed that everything he did would be controlled, certain and sure. Distracted, she noted that he had a supple body, vigorous and arresting. With his wicked smile and dark hair—a rogue wave spilling over his brow and shining like glass in the sunlight slanting through the windows—she thought he would have made the most handsome pirate.

Satisfied that the horse was in good health, he quickly saddled it up and slapped its flank before giving Catherine his full attention. Observing the soft flush on her cheeks, he raised a questioning eyebrow and studied her for a long, drawn-out moment. Catherine watched as a slow smile curved his lips. The sparkle in his eyes gradually evolved into a rakish gleam and she felt her flush deepen. She had no way of discerning the working of his mind or where his imagination wandered.

'There,' he said, 'you can take her out.'

In the yard John locked his hands together to accept Catherine's small, booted foot, and was not surprised at the agility she displayed when he raised her up to the saddle. Striding to his own mount, he swung himself up on to its back. It was a spirited stallion and John controlled him superbly. The lean, hard muscles of his thighs gripped the horse and he kept him on a tight rein to control his high-stepping prancing as they clattered out of the yard into the open countryside. Urging their horses into a lunging gallop, they crouched low over their necks, thundering over the snow-covered turf with ground-devouring strides. They rode at full speed, side by side, leaping low hedges in graceful unison. After a while they slowed their horses to a leisurely canter.

A lightening of spirits seemed to come over Catherine. She appreciated being away from the house if just for a little while. She was pleasantly aware of the emptiness of the scenery all around her, the smell of the crisp, cold air and the snow-covered ground. They rode over a humped-back bridge spanning a wide stream that tumbled on its way to its destination. The path they were following led on to open ground littered with large boulders. Deciding this would be a suitable place to eat, they paused by one of them and dismounted.

John unfastened a blanket from his saddle and unrolled it on the ground. Catherine sat gracefully on the blanket, resting her back against a boulder. Her face was rosy, her eyes bright from the ride. Removing her hat, she shook out her hair. John was completely transfixed by the heavy mass tumbling about her shoulders. It was thick and silken, shot through with tones of russet and gold and the gloss of good health. He could not hide that he liked what he saw and he found himself smiling with pleasure.

Forcing his mind to think of other things, he placed the basket of food between them and opened it, dipping in to find roast chicken, cheese, bread and butter and fruit. Spreading a cloth on the blanket, they ate in companionable silence, each content to gaze at their surroundings and appreciate the fact that they were here, away from the solemn atmosphere that prevailed at Oakdene. They talked and sometimes were silent, content just to be together, each aware of the bond that was growing between them. They talked of the past, of their childhoods and the people who had moulded and influenced their lives.

When they had eaten, John sat on the blanket close beside Catherine, resting his back against the boulder. A slow, lazy smile swept across his handsome face as his eyes passed with warm admiration over her shapely legs encased in breeches and riding boots stretched out in front of her. He watched her tuck a stray lock of hair behind her ear. Her face was in repose—vulnerable, thoughtful, like a child waiting for something exciting to happen.

In his experience with women—and his experience could not be truthfully termed lacking—he had been most selective of those he had chosen to sample. Yet it was difficult to call to mind one as delectable as the one he now scrutinised so carefully. Even now, even though she had been a married woman, having known her for several weeks and held her in his arms on occasion, he found there was a graceful naivety about Catherine Stratton that totally intrigued him.

'What are you thinking about?' he asked gently.

Catherine turned her head and found him studying her. 'Nothing too profound. Just things in general.'

'Care to tell me about them?'

'They're hardly worth discussing.' She sighed, her gaze taking in the panoramic view. 'This is a beautiful place,' she said, her gaze caressing the gentle rise and fall of the countryside.

He glanced at her, his arm resting on his knee. 'Are you missing Carlton Bray?'

'Yes—sometimes I do. Here, being close to London, everything is so different. At Carlton Bray if I wanted to disappear and be anonymous I could. Here I feel—visible.'

John smiled lazily. 'Careful, Catherine. You're beginning to reveal your insecurities. Do you feel you have the need to disappear?'

'Sometimes.'

'You are too warm and vitally alive. It would be a sin to hide yourself away.' Stretching out beside her, he ran the tips of his fingers across her lower lip. 'Tell me. How does a woman who has lived most of her adult life in a cold and dank castle on the Welsh Marches manage to have skin so soft?'

Her mouth opened against his fingertips. 'I am not old, John, so my skin is not aged. I think it is because I lived in a cold castle—although it was not always cold. In summertime, when the sun was hot, the castle was a relief in itself.'

'Was it, now?' he murmured as he continued to trace the outline of her mouth. Only a slight, momentary quiver of her jaw told him she was at all affected by what he was doing. All that passion just under the surface—what would happen if it were ever allowed to come out? He moved his hand to cradle her chin, and her hand moved as if to push it away, but stilled in the air, hesitant. 'What would it take for you to let your guard down now, Catherine?'

'I was not aware that my guard was up.'

'I have always prided myself on my self-control, but you are an expert at it. Would you mind if I kissed you again?'

She hesitated. 'I—I...'

'It shouldn't be too difficult. Why did you let me kiss you before?'

Her gaze was fixed on his mouth. 'I suppose when emotions are running high people do mad things.'

'And are your emotions running high now?'

'When I'm with you my emotions are always running high, even though I try to suppress them. You asked me why I let you kiss me.' Her lips curved in a slow smile. 'I wanted you to do it. I ignored all my instincts and let you do it without reservation, but then I told myself I must not be tempted again.'

'But you want me. You can't deny that.'

'I'm human, John. You've proved that.'

For a long moment John's gaze lingered on the elegant perfection of her glowing face, then settled on her entrancing green eyes. He wanted more than anything to snatch her into his arms to kiss that full, soft mouth until she was clinging to him, melting with desire. And then she totally surprised him by leaning forward and doing to him what he had been tempted to do to her. He could feel her desire and her apprehension as she kissed him gently, moulding her lips to his, touching them with the tip of her tongue. Her artless passion took his breath away. It was a kiss unlike any other. He could not remember being kissed like this before. Raising his hand, he pushed his fingers into her wealth of hair and cupped the back of her head.

The day had cast a spell on them and they had not the strength to escape it as they became lost in each other. They were each aware that they were completely alone. Raising his head, he looked down at her, smiling slightly as he stared into her eyes before allowing his gaze to travel, slowly, over every inch of her face. He was fascinated by the wisps of hair that clung to her flesh and how her pink tongue licked the moisture from her lips in an innocently sensual gesture. He felt heat pulsate through his veins and he could not look away. Again their lips met.

After a moment Catherine drew back a little and looked at him and he could feel the warm, beguiling sweetness of her soft breath on his skin. He could see her desire was as great as his own, but she seemed so very vulnerable, almost fragile. More than anything in the world John wanted at that moment to take her to bed. Had she then made the smallest seductive gesture—had she indicated that she was willing—he might have taken her quickly there and then, but this was not the place and honour, which dictated everything in his life, dictated his decision now.

Drawing in a deep breath, summoning the iron will that had made his reason the master of his emotions since he was a child, he released her. 'We must stop now, Catherine. I think I should let you go while I still can.' He took her chin between his thumb and forefinger and lifted it, forcing her to meet his steady gaze. His serious expression remained as he studied her upturned face. Her eyes were still languorous, her lips soft from his kiss. 'I want you—and you want me. Ever since I first laid eyes on you at Carlton Bray you have no idea how much I have wanted you. It cannot end here. I won't let it.'

Gathering the basket and the blanket from the ground, they swung up on to their horses, gathered their reins and road back to Oakdene.

When they parted, John stood and watched as Catherine strode towards the house and disappeared. Even when her body was no longer in sight he could see the flashing lights of her hair in the dying light of the sun. He watched spellbound until even that disappeared before turning back to his horse and thoughtfully heading towards Windsor. He murmured her name and it echoed through his mind over and over again, accompanied by the ache in his loins and the disturbing, haunting image of flashing green eyes and cascading honey-gold hair.

Over the following days John was occupied at Windsor with military affairs so Catherine did not see him, but the memory of the kiss was still warm and happy inside her.

It was December and very cold. Oakdene saw a steady number of visitors as Edward's physician and

friends came to see him. He had grown weaker since
Catherine's arrival and suffered small seizures, each
one leaving him more incapacitated than the last. In
his measured opinion, the physician held out little hope
of recovery.

When Blanche was alone with him, raised voices
could often be heard coming from the sick room. When
Blanche emerged on one such occasion her eyes were
glittering with anger.

'The man's a devil,' Blanche told Catherine, who
was hovering on the stairs, ready to go to her father's
aid should things get out of hand. 'He thinks he knows
everything. I can feel him watching me, hating me.
He knows he is finished and I will soon get what is
my due as his wife. It stings him to realise that I have
beaten him, after all.'

Catherine watched her go. Let Blanche think she
had beaten her father if that pleased her, but if she really thought she could get the better of him then she
was mistaken. The days were long gone when he would
concern himself with household matters. Since he had
become ill and taken to his bed, life slipped by for him
in a blur. But this one thing with Blanche was immediate and would not be put aside.

Catherine did not see the boy James, but she heard
his childish chatter and laughter sometimes. She was
tempted to seek him out in the nursery, but having no
wish to encounter Blanche she kept away. The nurse-
maid took him outside in the mornings and Catherine
would sit on her cushioned window seat and watch

them walk around the garden and sit a while before disappearing back into the house.

After another bitter altercation with her husband, Blanche had gone into town and was to remain overnight with friends. Snow had been falling since early morning and had begun to settle. Feeling restless and thinking she would benefit from some fresh air, Catherine made her way to the nursery. James was playing with a spinning top, watching it whirl over the carpet in a blur of bright colours, his dark eyes alight with excitement. Jenny was sewing in front of the fire. She looked up and smiled when Catherine entered.

'I've come to see James,' Catherine said, glancing at the little boy who was looking at her with childish interest. 'When I saw him last he had a tooth coming through. Is he better now?'

'Yes, he's much better, although he's fretful at having to stay indoors.'

'And who can blame him.' Catherine went to the child and smiled down at him, admiring his spinning top. His dark curly hair clung around his face. His eyes were grey, his jawline square—exactly like Thomas's, she thought, feeling an instinctive poignancy. She had no doubt that this was Thomas's son—the child that might have been hers. 'Teeth are nothing but trouble. Would you show me your new tooth, James?' He opened his mouth willingly, eager for her to see. 'Ah, there it is,' she said, peering inside. 'It's a fine tooth. See, it's snowing. It looks much more fun to be outside.' She looked at Jenny. 'Might I take him outside? You look as if you have plenty to occupy you.'

'I have. Master James grows out of his clothes so quickly I'm forever altering them. As you see he's still in skirts. It will be a relief when he's out of them. I haven't had time to take him outside yet, but I think it should be all right for you to take him—if you would like to.'

'Would you like that, James?' Catherine asked. 'We could make a snowman, if you like, and snowballs.'

His face was a delight to see. Jenny lost no time in dressing him in his outdoor clothes and little boots and mittens. As soon as they left the house James was off, running gleefully about the garden, kicking up the snow as he went. Holly bushes, bright with berries, and trees, their branches heavy with snow, stood sharp against the azure-blue sky and the sun shone on the glittering white unblemished gardens. The air was sharp and crystal clear and everything was still.

In no time at all the sound of shrill childish laughter rose and fell in paroxysms of uncontrollable mirth as they began to build the snowman. Together they rolled the bottom half of the body. The larger it got, the heavier it was to push. When it was halfway built, James made snowballs and threw them at Catherine, uncaring that his clothes were getting hopelessly wet. Leaving off rolling the snowman, Catherine made snowballs of her own and gently tossed them at him. Gazing up at her, he gave her a heart-stopping grin and threw another.

Chapter Seven

Having ridden from the city, it was into this setting that John appeared, being drawn to it by the ringing tones of laughter. He stared in astonishment to see Catherine sitting on the ground covered with snow, the child taking great delight in pelting her with snowballs, a ball of snow rolled to make the body of a snowman. Clearly it had proved too much for her.

Taking a moment to observe her, John felt his stomach churn. Seeing her like this, dishevelled, with her rich curtain of hair long and silky and every shade of autumn, almost took his breath away and he could not take his eyes from her.

She was magnificent. She turned her head to where he stood. He had appeared too suddenly for her to prepare herself, so he could almost sense the heady surge of pleasure she experienced on seeing him again, for it was stamped like an unbidden confession on her lovely face. For a long, joyous interval they held each other with their eyes, savouring the moment, enjoying afresh the powerful sexual force that sprang between them.

She held her head proudly, her green eyes burning up into his, showing neither alarm at his appearance or caring much for modesty. He was disturbed by the sight of her sitting in the snow, feeling a stirring of warmth in his loins. When he held out his hand, she took it and he hoisted her to her feet. She brushed the snow from her skirts with her hands. He noted how her eyes shone and how rosy her face.

'You look as if you're having a good time.' He watched a smile appear, lighting up her whole face, and John melted beneath the heat of it.

'We were indulging in happy playfulness—which is quite normal when it snows. It might be gone tomorrow. See—we're building a snowman, aren't we, James?'

'Yes,' squealed James, throwing another snowball at her.

With his hands on his hips, John inspected the ball of snow gravely, looking the picture of vastly amused male superiority. 'Is that the best you can do?' he said, unable to resist joining in the fun. 'It looks like a man's job to me.'

Catherine gasped, her look one of mock offence. 'How dare you say that. We haven't finished it yet.'

'I can see that. But I still say you need a man to roll it up. Permit me.' And without further ado he rolled the ball of snow a bit further.

James though it was hilarious to see him flounder

beneath the strain. Plonking her hands on her hips, Catherine gave John a look of comic disapproval. 'There, you see—it's not as easy as you think.'

John was not done. Determined to roll it a bit further and tensing his muscles, he rolled it until Catherine told him it was quite large enough, thank you, and if he left it where it was James would be able to see it from the nursery window. Standing back and slapping the snow off his gloves with a triumphant grin, he looked with admiration at the huge ball of snow.

'There you are. That is much improved. Do you not agree?'

Beckoning James to come and stand beside her, when she replied her voice was soft and very sweet. 'Yes, John. It certainly is,' she said with uncharacteristic meekness—and the next thing John knew, two pairs of hands, one large and one small, had hit him squarely on the chest and knees, catching him completely by surprise and sending him flying backwards to land spread-eagled in a snowdrift.

'Why, you—you hellions,' he cried with a bark of laughter as he struggled to get out of the drift.

'That,' she told him, joining in his laughter, 'was for arrogantly assuming that James and I are incapable of building our own snowman.'

'My pride is in ruins.' John laughed. Getting to his feet and brushing the snow off his clothes and hair, he knew he wasn't immune to the absolute exhilaration that came from being out of doors surrounded by snow—which he'd always hated before—while Catherine, her hair in a wet tangle about her shoulders, cheeks the colour of a bright red poppy, was a breathtaking marvel, with her huge jewel-bright green eyes and wide, laughing mouth.

'It's dangerous being within our range,' she shouted, handing James a snowball and making one for herself. 'We have excellent aims.'

'That does it. You'll pay for that,' John shouted as the snowballs hit him on the side of his head.

Scooping up some snow and moulding his own snowball, grinning broadly and with a dangerous gleam in his eyes, he purposefully advanced on them. Uncaring who might be watching, they cavorted about in the snow, shattering the quiet with their laughter. James squealed with excitement and ran away, while hoping John would chase him. Which he did, scooping the child up into his arms and tossing him playfully in the air before catching him, James's delighted laughter mingling with John's. Placing him back on his feet, John then turned his attention on Catherine.

'Oh, no—no, you don't,' she cried, beginning to back away and choking on her laughter. 'Stop it, John. You must be sensible about this. I've decided I don't like snowballs—'

'It's too late for that.' Suddenly John lunged and landed a direct hit on her shoulder. With a shriek, bent on revenge, she dipped her hands in the snow.

'You—you devil. I'll get you back for that. I swear I will.' And so saying, she quickly made another snowball and threw it at him before making a dash for it.

'And I'll teach you the folly of daring to provoke me,' John shouted after her, scooping up more snow and giving chase. James stood aside, jumping up and down with excitement and clapping his hands.

Encumbered by her skirts and the deep snow, Catherine pitched forward with a screech, landing face down in the snow. Rolling on to her back and laughing helplessly, she made an attempt to get to her feet, but James ran to her and sat on top of her, having the greatest time of his young life.

John, hands on hips and breathing heavily, stood looking down at them. 'Enough, you two,' he said, lifting James off an exhausted but laughing Catherine and helping her to her feet.

Reluctant to return to the house and end this pleasant interlude, she turned her attention to the more serious business of finishing the snowman. 'Don't think you're going to escape just yet,' she said.

'You mean there's more snowballing?'

'No. We have to give the snowman a face. Is that not so, James?'

'Yes,' he cried, running to the half-built snowman.

Catherine quickly rolled another ball of snow, smaller this time, for the head. John stood it on top of the large ball while Catherine collected twigs for its nose and mouth and stones for its eyes.

'There,' she said, standing back to admire their work. 'I think that's the finest snowman I've ever seen—don't you agree, James?'

James nodded in agreement, his crop of wet curls clinging to his cheeks.

'And now, young man,' Catherine said, taking James's hand, thinking he looked quite worn out but happy, 'I think we had better get you back to the house and out of those wet clothes.

John scooped the child up into his arms and the three of them made their way to the house.

Walking beside John, if Catherine had thought James would be subdued by his presence she was soon proved wrong. At first he had fixed him with dubious, uneasy glances, but John soon captivated his attention, possessing a natural ability to break down James's reserve. He seemed to have an easy rapport with him and it was quite a novelty to see him scooping up the snow and making snowballs, sending James into gales of laughter as they rolled about in the snow.

This new John was so surprising that Catherine could not restrain her amazement. She felt a tingling of exhilaration, drawn to him against her will by a compelling magnetism that radiated from his very presence. She looked at him as though for the first time and saw that, with his dark hair wet and ruffled and falling over his brow, he looked much younger and less formidable. For a moment she had the impression that he was little more than a boy himself. He did seem genuinely fond of James and he of him. When she managed to catch his eye there was so much laughter on his face that he seemed a long way removed from the serious-minded man she had come to know. It gave her an insight into a different side of him she was looking forward to knowing better.

'Really, John,' she said as they headed for the nursery. 'I am quite impressed. Never would I have believed you to be so good with children. I am pleased to see you do not view them as an encumbrance.'

'I like children. My brothers have four between them. Unfortunately I don't have the opportunities I would like to spend with them.'

'Perhaps that will be remedied when you have left the army. You seem to be such an expert that should you have children of your own in the future, I think you will be able to dispense with the services of a nurse.'

He smiled into her eyes. 'I'm not such an expert—or so patient. Where's Blanche, by the way? She's quite strict where James is concerned. I'm surprised she would let you bring him out to play in the snow.'

'She went into the city shortly after breakfast—before the snow made the roads worse. Father and Blanche argued before she left.' She sighed. 'I wish they wouldn't. She won't return until tomorrow.'

John's eyebrows rose with interest. 'Really? Then I think we should make the most of it. Tomorrow I go to Windsor for a few days. I'm then going down to Sussex. I promised my mother I would be there for Christmas. So tonight is my last night. Will you have supper with me?'

'Yes—yes—all right. That would be nice. I'll have Cook prepare something special.'

* * *

Catherine was delighted that John had suggested they dine together. Before she went down to supper she took time over her appearance. She was strangely excited about dining with him alone. The mere idea brought a familiar twist to her heart, that addictive mix of pleasure and discomfort that came over her every time she was with him, a sensation that somehow made breathing difficult and made her heart race as if she had been running. She arranged her hair, fluffing it here and there, and pinched her cheeks to an attractive pink and was half-ashamed, half-gratified at what she saw as an improvement. As she dabbed rosewater on her neck and wrists, a voice jeered from inside her, which she quelled. Why shouldn't she want to look nice? Wasn't it a woman's duty to herself?

Supper was a lovely, relaxed affair by the fireside in the parlour. It was served by Mrs Coleman, who brought them a bottle of claret from Edward's cellar, then left them alone. John told amusing tales of his exploits in the army over the years and Catherine was content to listen in fascination. Afterwards she suggested a walk outside before going to bed. The night was cold. They walked just a short way, their feet crunching on the snow. Reaching the end of the garden, she stopped and looked back at the house. John stood beside her.

'You look thoughtful. Memories?' His voice was quiet, his mood pleasant and attentive.

Catherine nodded and turned and looked at him, lifting her face to his. The light from the moon and the reflection off the snow added to its beauty and John felt it strike to the very soul of him.

'I was thinking of all the times I played in the gardens as a child. I loved spring in particular, when the trees and shrubs would burst into life. In summer they were a riot of roses and jasmine and honeysuckle. My mother was the gentlest, most caring of people and believed in the best in everyone. She would make a point of telling me the names of all the flowers and I would sit under that tree over there making daisy chains and lose myself in daydreams and wishes.'

'And what did you wish for?'

'That I would stay here for ever—and like every other little girl I wished that I would be pretty and that one day a prince would come and whisk me away and take me to live in a beautiful palace. The garden is an ideal place for a child to dream and play.'

'You must have been a happy child.'

'I was, but I didn't know anything else so I thought that was the way of things.'

When she turned and strolled on he walked beside her with a long, casual stride. They proceeded for several minutes in silence and then he paused.

'Tell me, Catherine, do you still dream?'

'Yes, but my dreams are not those of a child any more. I'm glad I managed to persuade Jenny to let me bring James out to play. I don't think he has much joy in his life and I know how much he enjoyed building the snowman—although see,' she said, pointing to the object of their efforts, 'already it's beginning to melt.'

'But you had fun. I'm sure James will remember it.'

'I would like to think so. I've only just found out about his existence and I am already concerned for his future. My father refuses to accept the child as his— and I have to say that he does resemble Thomas. So what is to be done?'

'I will see that she and James are taken care of— one way or another.' He looked down at her. 'You're trembling.'

'Yes, a little.'

'Are you cold?'

She twisted her head round and looked at him, unsmiling. 'No. It's your fault.'

'I have that effect on you?'

'Don't look so smug—but, yes, you do. You know, John, when you wrote informing me that you were bringing Thomas's body back to Carlton Bray, I didn't know what to think. I knew nothing about you. In fact, I was determined not to like you. It was no use. For the time we have been together I have seen a different man to the one I expected, a man who melted my resistance. And then you kissed me and scattered my wits.'

'It would seem you are confused about me, Catherine. I can see your dilemma.'

'Can you?' She believed he could. John Stratton had a razor-sharp perception of her. 'With everything that has happened of late, I have never been so unsure of myself. When I let you escort me to Oakdene

I unwittingly made more problems for myself than I bargained for.'

'And that scares you?'

'Yes, yes, it does.'

John watched her, both touched and faintly amused by her confession and aroused by her nearness. 'Do you fear me, Catherine?'

'No, not you,' she said quietly, feeling his eyes on her causing the colour in her cheeks to deepen. 'It's what you might do to me that I'm afraid of.'

Without a word he lifted his hands and tucked her cloak close about her neck to keep out the cold before drawing her into his arms. His mouth covered hers, moist, firm, lightly touching at first, then probing and demanding, and, as the ache spread to her bones, sensations that prolonged the exquisite torture, she wondered how long she could withstand him. When at last he lifted his mouth from hers, Catherine was trembling with awakened desire.

'John,' she whispered. 'I—'

He interrupted her in a deep, quiet voice. 'I like to hear you say my name and take you in my arms.'

Again his lips covered hers and he kissed her for a long time, tenderly, carefully, deliberately, holding back the urgent passion that possessed him. It was a restrained kiss, because he exercised the greatest control. Then he raised his head and their eyes met and held, touching hidden places and already imagining the possibility of a next time.

'I think we should return to the house,' he said, taking her hand.

They walked, holding hands like lovers, making no conversation. The moon shone down on them and only the faintest of breezes rustled through the empty branches of the trees, making time unimportant. Catherine looked at the house and it reminded her of the reasons for her being here, but on a night such as this she did not really want to think—either of the past or the future. It seemed that John felt the same, for he appeared content to simply be there, with her.

I am happy at this moment, Catherine thought contentedly. And then, without wanting to, she wondered, *Will I always feel so with him?*

No matter what events had led up to this moment, she was happy and everything seemed changed between them—the past and all its hardships vanished like mist clearing before the rising of the sun.

When he would have drawn her into his arms once more, she stepped away. 'I must go and say goodnight to Father—and to make sure he has everything he needs.'

This she did. Entering her father's room, she found him on the verge of sleep. After ensuring a maid was on hand should he wake, she left him, intending to go to her own chamber.

'Catherine.'

There was a movement behind her and the voice that spoke her name was deep, warm and loving. She closed her eyes, feeling the dizzy aura of him, unable to resist it. Wanting to savour the sound of it, she didn't turn, although she could imagine his eyes in the candlelight shining with an expression she would like to think he had given to no woman but her.

She heard him come closer, his footsteps almost soundless on the thick carpet, then he was directly behind her, so close she could feel the warmth of him on her back. Then his arms snaked around her waist. He pulled her back and she sank into him, unable to resist. He held her to his chest and buried his head into the curve of her neck, his lips warm, caressing her flesh. Sighing, she began to melt, feeling languorous magic drift over her.

'Mmm,' he breathed. 'You smell of roses.'

'And you, my lord, smell of brandy and fresh air and manly things'

'Do you mind?' he asked, his teeth gently nibbling her earlobe.

'Not in the slightest,' she whispered, a thrill of excitement tingling along her nerves. 'I like it. It's a pleasant smell.'

'Are you tired?'

She shook her head. 'I should be after our fun and games earlier in the snow. But I don't feel like going to bed just yet,' she said softly, covering his hands at her waist with her own.

'Neither do I—at least, not alone.' His arms tightened about her and his voice was husky. 'Have you the slightest idea how much I want you, Catherine? Will you not turn round and tell me you feel the same?'

She turned slowly, shivering slightly, for she felt the power of his masculinity, the strong pull of his magnetism, which she knew was his need for her, wrap itself about her. His face was all shadow and planes in the soft light. She felt a hollow ache inside as he gazed down at her. He framed her face with his hands and bent to brush her lips with his, a mere whisper of a caress, gently, barely discernible. Raising his head, he took her face in his hands and splayed his fingers over her cheeks, looking into the liquid depths of her eyes.

'You're incredibly lovely, Catherine. Do you know how lovely you are? Come to bed with me.'

She paused, considering the question. What would it mean to be alone with him? Should she be afraid of that moment, afraid of what would happen between them—and the surrender for which, after Thomas, she was wary of? The fear she was feeling grew sharper. What madness was it that made her feel she knew this man at all? When he again took her lips, in an instant her fear of him dissolved.

She moaned with pleasure. Did it matter that they weren't wed when his mouth, his hands, his powerful body were demanding things from her that she knew she could give him? She was a widow, no longer a virgin—although she had no tender memories of what Thomas had done to her. If anything at all, memories of his rough handling were enough to put her off having any other man in her bed for all time. She had never experienced the glorious sensations she felt when John held her. As she looked at him now, something in those brilliant blue eyes made her catch her breath. Once more her body flamed with passion and for once she did not care. She had so long been denied this intimacy with a man, and had determinedly kept her mind from any such feelings, that she now recklessly welcomed it.

Taking her silence as acquiescence, he took her hand and led her to his bedchamber. She wanted him desperately and just now nothing else mattered. She went with him willingly, knowing it was wrong—and yet she argued with herself as he drew her inside.

'Wait,' he said as she was about to move further into the room. 'If you are not comfortable with this, you need not stay with me. I ask nothing of you but to be with you, Catherine. I will do nothing that you do not allow.'

Feeling surprisingly calm, Catherine remembered how different it had been when she had married Thomas out of duty and obligation, which, since meeting John, she would toss into the teeth of the wind to be blown away. Tonight she was her own person and sure of herself. John wanted her and she knew he spoke the truth, and hugged the knowledge and the thought to her as a talisman against the past.

'I have thought about it,' she said. She wanted to know if she would find the experience as distasteful as she remembered. She wanted to know—to feel that there was more. 'There was nothing loving about my relationship with Thomas. His treatment of me was harsh. My memory of the times he took me to his bed is of pain. I thought that was all there was. I thanked God every day that for the short time we were together he left me alone. It was clear he did not see me as desirable—I thanked God for it. For the first time, since I met you, I know it doesn't have to be like that.'

John took her into his arms and kissed her soft mouth again. Her lips trembled and then finally parted helplessly, allowing him full rein. Making the most of his plunder, he kissed her long and deep. It was a kiss so poignant, so filled with sensual promise, that she found herself melting against him, her senses scattered in a storm of unexpected desire. Her tongue flirted with his as her fingers drifted over the muscles of his shoulders.

Raising his head, he gazed down at her upturned face. 'I want you in my bed, Catherine. I want to see you. I want to touch you, to taste you.' His lips found hers once more, gently caressing before slowly moving to her cheek and down the column of her throat to the tender hollow where her pulse beat beneath her skin. And then, with slow deliberation, he began to undress her, his burning eyes devouring every inch of her exposed flesh. When she stood in her chemise the firelight betrayed her beauty through the filmy cloth, showing the slender curves of her body in silhouette. His hands stroked down her arms and back again, caressing her shoulders. He felt her tremble beneath his touch. His clever fingers continued with their caress, setting the pace to slowly arouse and seduce until she had no will of her own under his skilful hands.

He drew back, his eyes dark with passion as he studied her intently. 'Do you fear it, Catherine?'

'A little.

'Then don't. Ever since I kissed you that first time I've been fighting against my need for you.' He put his fingers beneath her chin and turned her face up to his. 'I am nothing like Thomas and I feel a need for you to trust me. I will give you pleasure. It is my wish to erase your memories of Thomas's harsh treatment of you. Do you trust me to do that?'

'I trust you to try.'

Catherine was aware of him touching her skin once more, aware of every caress with his lips, his fingers, and the moment his arms were about her, her almost naked body caught against the hard pressure of his body. Her passion exploded into fire. The attraction between them had been denied for too long. Her body became a flame as it moved against his and desire ravaged her senses. She felt his hot breath on her flesh and experienced the same rush of helplessness as before when he held her, the same yielding softness. The image of Thomas which had fleetingly occupied her mind was gone in a blur of savagery and passion as John's mouth ground down on to hers, his lips possessive and demanding, holding her warm and pliant body utterly captive. His kiss was devastating and a shudder ran through her to delight him.

Taking her hand, he led her to the bed where she stretched out on the covers. John knelt beside her and raised her up. Holding her tight against him, he kissed her throat before releasing her and getting off the bed to divest himself of his clothes. When he joined her she raised up on her knees and pulled the curtains, shutting out the light from the candles and leaving just the bottom of the bed exposed so they could see the glow of the fire across the room.

Beside him once more, Catherine passed her eyes over his body with admiration. It was strong and hard, his muscles clearly defined. With his hands on her shoulders he slipped the flimsy material of her chemise down her arms, then this final garment was quickly removed and floated to the floor. Stretching out alongside her, he gathered her close, the warmth of his body pressed full against the coolness of her own. The heat of his lips made Catherine lose touch with reality. The attraction which had always been between them blazed into something more profound. It was impetuous, an abandoned sensual action, but impossible to halt or deny.

The feel and the taste of him filled her soul. His mouth moved to circle her breasts, kissing each in turn until her nipples hardened. Consumed by him, she gasped in pleasure as his mouth moved down over her ribs, his tongue teasing the taut skin of her stomach and the soft swell of her hips. When he pressed his mouth to her softness she threw back her head and her fingers laced through his hair as she abandoned herself to the waves of pleasure that expanded and mounted until finally pulsating into release. She could not stop his hands from roving. Her body was unchartered territory and her flesh was satiny soft and quivered under his inquisitive touch. A need began to grow inside her as his caresses grew bolder. It was a hollow feeling that ached to be filled. She felt on the threshold of some great and already overwhelming discovery.

John took control, rolling her on to her back and taking his weight on his elbows so that he might look down at her and watch the play of emotions on her face and see the darkness of her eyes. For a moment, a small lance of sanity seemed to make her pause and gape at her behaviour. She was like a crazy woman, writhing on the bed in her father's house with a man who was not her husband. She was shocked, but only for a moment, for in the next John was raising her hips to accommodate him. The moment he penetrated her silken heat, finding solace in the pulsating softness of her body, their shocked gasps of pleasure were as one.

There was no shame or degradation as there had been with Thomas, no humiliation, only an intoxicating heat that pulsed through every inch of her body as he filled her and claimed her with thorough possession. With masterly precision he moved within her with utmost care and, with each thrust, their rhythm was matched with ardour. She clung to him, her fingernails digging into his back, their crescents unconsciously marking him as the abandonment went on, forcing her to forget everything but assuagement as he brought her to peak after peak of emotion she had never known existed. She was almost delirious with the new sensations and the powerful response of her own body. She was conscious of an unfamiliar heat inside her as he began to move gently and slowly, seductively initiating her into the arts of love.

John's body was huge and powerful, wonderful and glistening with sweat above her, his eyes dark with passion. The expanding pleasure, which she had never experienced before, made Catherine writhe and arch her hips against his as she allowed herself to be carried away again and again to the realms of ecstasy. She was unable to believe the delicious sensation of closeness as their bodies strained together. A small cry broke from her lips as the aura burst around them, bathing them in pulsating waves of pleasure.

When it was over Catherine's senses were in absolute disintegration. They lay together, arms and legs entwined as they drifted up from the nether regions where their passion had sent them. She had never been cherished in a man's tender embrace, or felt the singing in her blood as desire surged through her veins. John pulled the covers over them against the chill. The languor following their lovemaking was still with Catherine and she snuggled close to him, their legs entwined. Remembered caresses and murmured endearments added to her contentment. She stirred and opened her eyes to find John propped up on one elbow, staring down at her face which was delightfully flushed, her eyes liquid bright. She stretched her arms languorously above her head. Her breasts rose, their rosy peaks up-tilted and beckoning.

'I don't suppose Thomas told you how beautiful you are,' John said softly, his lips sliding along her arm, his tongue gently teasing her flesh.

'I don't think Thomas ever saw me,' she answered, remembering Thomas's fumbling and groping and the degradation and humiliation she had felt afterwards, so different from what she was feeling now.

He gently swept a lock of her hair from her face and tucked it behind her ear. 'And how do you feel?' he asked, looking at her, at her eyes wide and filled with a confused assortment of emotions.

Catherine didn't reply at once. How could she tell him that she was shaken by the force of what had happened between them—and shocked by the primitive intensity of emotions he had released inside her that had made her respond like some shameless wanton from the streets? She could not believe the delicious sensations of closeness and satisfaction.

'I never realised making love could be like that. I have to say that it exceeded anything I could have imagined. I feel relieved,' she murmured as a sense of well-being wrapped around her. All she wanted now was to sink into the bed against him and rest until it was time to repeat the wonderful experience.

The night seemed endless as they made love until just before dawn. Catherine lifted her head from John's chest, having slept for a while. He had kept his arms and one leg thrown over her to keep her possessively close to him. Memories of what had taken place came flooding back. Unable to move, she felt the heat of her blushes cover her whole body. She studied his face, relaxed in sleep. A lock of his dark hair dipped over his brow. Her feelings for him overwhelmed her. Remembered caresses and whispered endearments added to her contentment. She was hardly able to believe he was her lover, that he had made her feel like a woman at last simply by making love to her.

She was suddenly conscious of the time they had spent behind the locked door and that the servants would soon be about. Trying not to wake him, she slowly eased her way to the edge of the mattress. At her movement John stirred. His eyes opened. There was such tenderness in their dark depths that her heart felt it would burst with her emotions.

'Are you abandoning me so soon?' he murmured. His arms slid around her waist and he pulled her to him, his lips kissing her throat. She gasped as his hand moved down across her stomach to her thighs. 'It's early. We have plenty of time before I have to leave for Windsor.'

Unable to deny him, she snuggled into him. His lips moved across her shoulder to her breast and his tongue teased its rosy peak. As his hand stroked the curve of her spine, she felt her blood answering in response, until she was consumed with a need that matched his own.

Eventually, fulfilled, they finally slept once more.

* * *

When Catherine awoke John was beside the bed, already dressed and ready to leave. With a yawn she stretched her body, raising her arms above her head. Excitement leapt into John's eyes as he watched her, his eyes falling on the smooth roundness of her breasts, the gleaming shoulders, the exquisite length of her legs and the provocative roundness of her hips.

'You are without doubt the most glorious woman I have ever seen,' he murmured.'

He bent to kiss each of her breasts once more and then his mouth moved upwards until it reached hers. Still dazed and enchanted with the realisation that the lovemaking had been a sensuous, wondrous experience, she reached for him, unconsciously yearning upwards towards him. Her smile was tilted, her expressive eyes deliberately full of flirtatious mischief.

'No more, my love,' he whispered softly against her lips. 'Though God knows it wouldn't take long for my loins to recover with your sweetness beneath me.'

'Then stay.'

'We will be together again very soon and the prospect of that alone gives me the strength to wait. I have business in London and I'll call on the way back to Windsor. Dear God, but you don't know what you do to me, Catherine. You dazzle my senses, but I intend to leave you now with the pleasure of this first time still warm within you.'

With a kiss and a promise to return later, he left her then, only the familiar scent of his body lingering on the sheets. She was too inexperienced to know whether this was arrogant masculine talk or not and she didn't care. He had brought her to an awareness of her deeply hidden passions. With a new maturity born out of the night past, she accepted everything he said as the way she herself felt.

Blinking the lingering slumber out of her eyes, she flushed as the memories came rushing back. A rosy hue crept into her cheeks when she remembered the incredibly wanton things they had done. They had shared the most intimate of experiences and her body still tingled with their lovemaking. Even though the physical part of him had gone from her, the essence of him remained. There wasn't an inch of her that he hadn't touched or tasted as he had aroused her body with such skilful tenderness and shattered every barrier of her reserve. The night had held a thousand exquisite and unexpected pleasures for them both. With a sigh she stretched with languid contentment, thinking of him and the extraordinary things that had happened to her, to her body, when she had been in his arms.

But what now? she thought. What did she want—for she knew there would never be any peace of mind for her as long as John Stratton remained on earth? Time and distance were of no consequence, for he was already in the heart and soul of her and there he would remain.

Chapter Eight

As John rode towards Windsor, his thoughts turned to Catherine and the singular pleasure of taking her into his bed. He had been assailed by doubts before he had done so. Because of Thomas's harsh treatment of her he had been afraid that she would reject him. But she had come to him willingly, almost as if she wanted to erase the damage Thomas had done her and reassure herself that not all men were like him. John had known he wanted her from the moment he'd looked into those mesmerising green eyes. It had started then and strengthened the more time they spent together.

He had thought it would take considerable patience and sympathetic handling for him to build a relationship with her and it surprised him how willing she had been and that what they had done had not been the horror she had feared. She had responded hesitantly at first, but then she had warmed to him and welcomed his attentions, opening herself to him. He held a certain pride that she had not found the experience distasteful.

But what a terrible burden she had carried throughout her years at Carlton Bray with no one to help her,
disguising her fears and existing behind a barrier of
self-possession and competency. Thomas might not
have loved her, but he could not be forgiven his cruel,
thoughtless treatment of her. He had taken her for his
wife and she had deserved better.

He could only marvel at how much she had lowered
her defences toward him, like a wild horse that gentled
only to his touch. It was no small honour, for he knew
how reticent she had been towards him. Even now, he
could feel her vulnerability and it made him tremble
inside to see how much she trusted him when he wasn't
even sure if he could trust himself. Once he had won
her confidence she had responded to his lovemaking
with a violence that had startled them both. He was
completely absorbed in her and he told himself she
was the best thing he had ever found.

As Catherine went about her duties, she had never
thought it possible to be so happy, to feel such wonderful elation glowing inside her. The fear that she
might be with child crossed her mind and part of her
yearned to be with child, John's child, but how would
she explain it? Common sense told that she was wrong
to have gone to his bed, but she found that, when she
was with him, common sense played no part. She enjoyed feeling his hard body pressed to hers and experiencing the intimacy only two people who are strongly
attracted to each other can ever really know. When she

thought of the night they had spent together, she smiled and hugged herself, wondering how she could contain her happiness until she saw him again.

He had not said he loved her, but he must feel something for her. This comforting theory produced in her a mood of indulgence and gaiety. It was December already and she began to think about Christmas, as it had been when her mother was alive. Not since she was a young girl had there been such a bright sparkle in her eyes and a soft flush on her cheeks. Unfortunately her happiness was not to last.

It was mid-morning and Catherine went to the nursery to see James. He was seated on a chair near his bed, his short legs dangling over the edge of the seat. He kicked them idly back and forth as Jenny busied herself with tidying the room.

'Hello, James,' Catherine said. 'Did you enjoy yesterday, playing in the snow?'

His eyes lit up and he nodded shyly. 'I liked building the snowman and throwing the snowballs. Can we do it again?'

Catherine laughed. 'When it snows some more I don't see why not.' She looked at Jenny, who was disappearing into the adjoining room, a pile of linen in her arms. 'I thought I'd come and see if everything is all right, Jenny, with Blanche being away.'

'Yes, my lady,' she called. 'Master James has had his breakfast. We're going to draw some pictures when I've sorted out this laundry.'

'Then perhaps I can join you. I have to go and check on my father and then I'll come back. I like drawing and I'd like to see what James can draw.' She smiled at the dark-haired child. He really was adorable. Blanche must be very proud of him. 'Would you like that, James? Perhaps we can draw and colour a snowman since we can't go outside.'

Nodding his head enthusiastically, he slid off the chair.

Catherine left James building some wooden bricks into a tower, excited that she was going to return to play with him. She sighed, feeling sorry for the child. Her father refused to let him have the run of the house so he spent most of his time confined to the nursery.

She sighed inwardly on entering her father's room, pausing on the threshold, momentarily overcome by the closeness of the room. To ward off the cold a fire blazed in the hearth. Her father was sitting up in bed, swaddled in blankets. She found it hard to hide her shock at his appearance. The pallid flesh and shrunken eyes and sparse white hair covering his skull gave his face the appearance of a death mask.

'How are you feeling today, Father? No worse, I hope?' He was alone, the servant who tended him having gone to the kitchen to fetch him a cup of ale.

'Much the same,' he mumbled. 'I'm dying—I know it, so don't tell me I look well—but the good Lord keeps me hanging on. I like to keep the curtains pulled round the bed to keep out the draughts. I feel the cold in my bones.'

'Yes—well—that's hardly surprising. It's very cold outside. Is Blanche back yet?'

'No, not yet. I expect she'll be back any time.'

Catherine was aware that the door was being pushed slowly open. Thinking it was the servant returning with her father's ale, she didn't turn round immediately. It was only when she heard her father's sharp intake of breath that she did so. It was James, who, unbeknown to Jenny and hoping Catherine would change her mind and take him outside to build another snowman, had followed her. He peeked round the door and stepped into the room. Catherine tried to step between them so she blocked her father's view, but she was too late.

Edward's face worked. 'Get him out,' he spat, tiny flecks of spittle at the edges of his mouth. 'Get him out,' he repeated, his lips drawn back from his teeth in a snarl, rising up from the pillows, a maddening rage filling his eyes. 'I won't have him in my sight. Look what his mother's done. Brought shame on us all— shame, I tell you.' His hands gripped the sheets, furious at his inability to rise.

He fell back, his skin sheened with sweat. Afraid he was going to have a seizure, Catherine hurried to him and tried to calm him. By the time she turned back to the door, James had disappeared. Deeply concerned, she called for someone to sit with her father while she went to check on James. For as long as she lived she would never forget the look of fear on the child's face. Jenny looked up when she entered the nursery. There was no sign of James.

'Where is he, Jenny? Where is James?'

'I don't know, my lady,' Jenny replied, looking nonplussed. 'I thought he was with you.'

'He followed me to my father's room. Unfortunately he's not in the best of spirits this morning and I think he upset James. I'll go and look for him. He can't be far away.'

Catherine searched all the chambers on the upper floor, looking behind curtains and doors, anywhere she could think a small child could hide, but there was no sign of him. Rallying the servants to join in the search, she called his name again and again, trying to keep her voice calm so as not to alarm him more than he already was. She searched downstairs and along the corridors in the domestic quarters, but to no avail. No one had seen the child. The kitchen was the last place she looked. According to Mrs Coleman he loved the kitchen. Red coals glowed in the gigantic hearth and an orange light flickered on the copper pans hung on the walls. She searched the pantries and wash house at the back of the house, but James was nowhere to be seen.

As she stood in the hall, wondering where to look next, the door opened and Blanche swept in, having returned from her trip to London. In good spirits she removed her bonnet and placed it on the hall table before turning her attention to Catherine. Seeing the stricken look on her face, she walked towards her.

'Catherine—what is it? Has something happened? Is it Edward?'

Pulling herself together, Catherine shook her head.

Her expression of mingled guilt and dismay took a moment to penetrate. 'No, Blanche. It's James. Don't get alarmed, but he's gone missing. He can't be far away.'

There was a moment of frozen stillness, of utter clarity. 'Missing? What do you mean—missing? How can he go missing? Have you lost him?'

'I went to the nursery to see him and he followed me when I left. He—he followed me into Father's room…'

Blanche paled as she clutched at the frayed edges of her control. 'He actually went into Edward's room? My God! James must have been terrified. He always said there was something horrid in that room. He was right.' She looked stricken and was twisting her hands in anxiety. Her eyes flew round the hall and to the stairs, as if expecting to see her son at any moment. 'How could you let him wander like that? He never leaves the nursery unless he's with me or Jenny. You should have watched him, made sure he was safe. You should have known I didn't want him anywhere near Edward. He has to be somewhere in the house. Where have you looked?'

'Everywhere. I cannot imagine where he might be.'

'Have you looked outside?'

She shook her head. 'No—but I will.'

'He can't have gone far. I'll check the house again while you check the stables. He likes to look at the horses so he might have wandered round there.'

Instructing the servants to continue searching the house and grounds, Catherine hurried to the stables. Informing the grooms that James was missing, they separated to join in the search. After a thorough look inside the stables she emerged, just as John was dismounting, having ridden from London. Alarmed at seeing her so distraught, he went to her.

'Catherine? What on earth has happened?'

Quickly she explained, telling him that they had searched everywhere, but he seemed to have disappeared into thin air. Her eyes were wide, fixed in horror on the agony of losing James. 'He followed me into Father's room. Oh, John! He was so frightened. I couldn't go after him straight away because I thought Father was about to have a seizure. When I went to the nursery, Jenny hadn't seen him. I've looked everywhere. I can't think where he can have gone.'

John seized Catherine by the shoulders and forced her to look at him. 'Look at me,' he ordered, waiting until she did so, ignoring the fear in her eyes. 'We will find him. He's a child—probably hiding in the most unlikely of places. I'm sure he'll come out of hiding when he's ready. In the meantime we'll do another search of the house. Surely if he'd let himself out of the house someone would have seen him. Think of what you know about the house—from a child's perspective. If anyone can find him, you can.' He squeezed her shoulders gently to reinforce his words, forcing himself to ignore the panic-stricken grief in the green depths of her eyes.

She looked at him in shock. His eyes were hard, his face implacable, his fingers hard as they gripped her shoulders. Doubtless he, too, thought she was responsible. She pulled back out of his grasp, trying to draw on her thoughts and remember when she had been a child and played hide and seek with her mother.

With a decision came calm. If Blanche blamed her for James's disappearance, then there was little she could do to alter that. But she could do all in her power to find him.

'Let's go back to the house. He may have been found already. If not, I'll try to remember where I used to hide as a child.'

Blanche was weeping hysterically when they entered. She was circling the hall, her body gaining speed and agility from her intense distress. Seeing Catherine, she ran towards her.

'Where is he? Have you found him?' She could not hide the note of despair and desperation in her voice or the lines of strain around her mouth as tears coursed down her cheeks. 'What have you done with him?' she cried, surging towards Catherine.

John hastily intervened before Blanche could reach her. Grasping her wrists, he half-led, half-dragged her to a chair. 'Blanche, it is not Catherine's fault that James is missing,' he said in her defence. 'Everyone is doing their best to find him—and find him we will.'

Blanche let out another wail of distress, covering her face with her shaking hands.

'Stop it, Blanche,' Catherine said sharply. 'You are hysterical. You have to focus—think of James.'

Blanche looked up at her through her tears. 'James is all I ever think about. He is all I have. I cannot bear to think something might have happened to him. All I can see is his little face, stark with fear—brought on by that—that monster who calls himself my husband.'

Catherine's chest felt clogged and she was struggling to breathe. Turning away, she walked across the hall, ignoring the hovering servants all waiting to be told what to do next. Swallowing past the hard constriction in her throat, she tried not to think of James, all alone somewhere and frightened, James, who had been running around so happily in the snow yesterday. He would be shrunk into himself somewhere, confused and scared. But where? Where would he go to hide?

'I'll go through the house again,' she said to Blanche, trying hard not to show the fear that was almost paralysing her. 'I might have overlooked something.'

She went up the stairs, with John at her side, and along the corridor to the furthest part of the house. Together they did another thorough search of the rooms with no success. When they stood outside her father's room Catherine stopped and looked thoughtfully at the door. She turned to John.

'Have you thought of something,' he asked, frowning down at her.

'We've looked everywhere, but we haven't looked in Father's room. James disappeared when my attention was on Father—I thought he was about to have one of his turns. If, by any chance, James is still in there, he'll be too frightened to come out. And if Father sees him he'll be furious. Come in with me and keep Father occupied while I search.'

Together they entered the room. Her father's eyes were closed, his head back on the pillows. Thankfully he was asleep. Catherine strained her ears and her eyes. She was just about to move further into the room when she heard a small voice say, 'I'm here.'

'Oh, thank goodness,' Catherine rejoiced. It was not simply that James had lost his way, but naked fear born out of blind panic on hearing her father's voice raised in anger. The voice had come from behind one of the tapestries close to the door. The bed had its curtains partially pulled round so the figure in the bed couldn't see the tapestry.

Suddenly the fabric was thrown back at one corner and, with a small cry, James stumbled out and began to cry when he saw Catherine. He rushed over to her and clutched at her legs. The eyes that he raised to her face were wide and stark with terror. Moved immeasurably by his distress, Catherine bent down and swept him into a comforting hug. The knot in her chest loosened a little.

'It's all right, James,' she said, forcing down her panic as she carried him out of the room and pinning a reassuring smile to her face. 'Everything is all right. Your mother is looking for you—we've all been looking for you, when all the time here you are.'

Snivelling, he dragged his sleeve over his face, his eyes large and awash with tears. 'I ran away. I didn't like that nasty man. He frightened me.'

'Did he? I'm sorry about that, James. But that man is not very well. That is why he shouted. He wouldn't like to think he had frightened you."

His little mouth trembled violently. 'He did. I don't like him. Where's Mummy?'

'She's here—see,' Catherine said, turning him towards Blanche, who was hurrying towards them.

Blanche snatched the child out of Catherine's arms and hugged him close, her tears mingling with her son's. Without a word she climbed the stairs to the nursery. Her sobs could be heard until the nursery door closed behind her.

Catherine watched them go before turning to John, who had emerged from her father's room and closed the door.

'He must have crawled behind the tapestry when I was distracted. Poor little mite. Father must seem like a monster to him. I hope he won't remember this, but somehow I think he won't forget.'

'He's safe now, thank God. He gave us all a fright.'

Catherine slowly made her way to the stairs. John followed. They didn't speak until they were in the parlour. Taking it upon himself, John went to the dresser and poured a generous glass of wine. He took it to her.

'Sit down and drink this.'

She sat, but did not take the wine.

Taking her hand, he gave her the glass. 'Drink it. I insist. This past hour has been an ordeal. A judicious measure has the power to release impossible tensions.

It will help to relax you.' He sat across from her, watching her.

In no mood to argue, she took a swallow, feeling its warmth radiate through her. 'For a time I was truly worried that we wouldn't find him. I can't believe how angry Father was when he saw James—and James was so frightened. It must be so difficult for Blanche.'

Her voice died away as the tension of the past hour began to leave her. Colour returned to her face and her eyes were bright. After a while John got to his feet.

'I have to leave, Catherine. I have commitments at Windsor that will keep me employed for several days. I'll try to get back when I can.'

Catherine walked with him to the parlour door where they paused. John caught her chin in his hand and kissed her, then he put his arms around her and held her to him.

'I'll miss you,' he murmured, burying his lips in her tangled hair.

Catherine closed her eyes and rested against his broad chest. How safe she felt in his embrace. Luxurious weak tears of exhaustion and relief ran down her cheeks, and her shoulders slumped. John held her close and stroked her back. After a long time, when her tears had ceased, he released her and left.

The repercussions from the morning had still to come.

Catherine hadn't seen Blanche again the day before. She'd remained in the nursery with James. The following morning Blanche lost no time in going to Edward and, much to Catherine's dismay, she heard angry words exchanged before Blanche emerged and stormed to the nursery, before returning to her chamber and closing the door.

Sensing that something was dreadfully wrong, unable to contain her concern Catherine knocked on her door and entered, surprised to find Blanche packing clothes into a trunk. She looked up when Catherine entered, but did not stop what she was doing.

'Catherine! Have you come to gloat?'

'No, Blanche, I wouldn't do that. I would have to be deaf not to have heard your altercation with my father. What happened?'

'You must have heard. Your father's illness and inability to get out of bed has triggered a fury of frustration in him, that much is clear—to such an extent that he has terrified my son half to death. He has to vent his fury for allowing James to stray into his room and it's fallen on me.'

'But—what are you doing?'

'I'm doing what I should have done years ago. Leaving. He's turned me out.'

'Because of James?'

'Yes.' Blanche paused with what she was doing and looked steadily at Catherine. 'You know, don't you, that James is Thomas's child?'

'Yes, I do. When I first saw James I suspected it—he looks like Thomas. Father confirmed it. Did Father know at the time that after Marston Moor Thomas was with you in York?' When Blanche looked at her sharply, she smiled. 'Father told me that, too.'

'He found out later. He reproached me most severely for my breach of duty. I thought he would cast me out there and then, but he took me back on the condition that I never met, spoke or wrote to Thomas. I adhered to his demand—I didn't even know of Thomas's demise until Edward got back from the north and told me. Any vain hope of forgiveness was shattered when I discovered I was with child after we had been together in York. He knew it couldn't possibly be his.'

'But he let you stay.'

'Yes, but he told me that I must not entertain any expectation of a fair settlement from him when he died, for I would not get a brass farthing.'

'I'm sorry. That must have been hard for you to accept.'

'It was. And imagine how I felt when he took pleasure in telling me that Thomas's last words were of you.'

'I'm sorry about that, too—although I find it difficult to believe. You loved him, didn't you, Blanche?'

'As much as it is possible for a woman to love a man.'

'Blanche, did you tell him about James?'

She shook her head. 'No. As I said, I kept my promise to Edward and didn't inform Thomas—which I now regret. It is the worst thing I have ever done.'

Catherine's bright gaze rested on Blanche, seeing her as if for the first time. A handsome woman with brown eyes quicker to harden than to soften with warmth, the wide mouth curved for laughter, but held too tight. She knew how much Blanche had loved Thomas and saw clearly how this love had affected all the years since she had met him. Catherine could now understand Blanche's bitterness and her continuance of it.

'You should not have made the promise to my father that you would have nothing further to do with Thomas. You should have gone to him. He had a right to know his son.' She was tempted to tell Blanche that Thomas had known about his son, that her father had told him, but she thought it was best left for now. John would tell her when the time was right. 'I won't pretend our marriage was anything other than tolerated. You of all people know the truth of that. I am certain Thomas would have made provision for James had he known about him.'

'I know that now. But what would you have done, Catherine, had I appeared at Carlton Bray with Thomas's son in my arms?'

'I would not have turned you away. I would have given you shelter until something could be worked out. Where will you go?'

Blanche lowered her eyes and continued with her task. 'I'm not sure. What I do know is that I have to get James away from here with the hostile atmosphere coming out of Edward's room daily. I will not have my son raised in fear. I'll take a few things with me and send for the rest when I'm settled.'

'I'll see that they are ready. Will you go to your parents?'

For the first time Blanche's certainty slipped. White-faced, she stared at Catherine for a moment until something inside her seemed to collapse in the face of defeat. All at once she seemed smaller. Her expression was sad. 'No. I can't do that. They are old and not at all well. After losing their money and Murton House they are living with relatives on their charity. I cannot in all fairness enforce my situation on them. I'll take the coach and send it back when I reach my destination.'

'There's no hurry. Father isn't going anywhere and I prefer to ride. Besides, the coach I travelled in from Carlton Bray is still here. The driver, who has family in the city, is in no hurry to go back. You will let me know where you are staying, won't you?'

She nodded. 'I'm sorry for what I said yesterday when James went missing. It's wasn't your fault—but I'm so protective of him that I couldn't bear it if anything happened to him.'

'There's no need to apologise. These things happen and I understand.'

'Jenny told me how you took James out to play in the snow while I was away—that John was here. He loved it and couldn't wait to tell me about it. It was what he needed—to run around and build a snowman, to play silly games like normal children. If I didn't have James, I would stay and fight for my rights. As it is I don't have any. I have to go for his sake. He's usually such a solemn little boy. He's quickly learned to make himself quiet and still so as not to annoy Edward.'

'I am sorry for your unhappiness, Blanche,' Catherine said with difficulty. She now saw so many aspects to Blanche she had never seen before. 'I know we have our differences, but I don't like to see you crushed.'

'I am not crushed.' Blanche's chin went up. 'I endure—I *will* endure.'

'Of course you will. James is a charming little boy and we had such a lovely day in the snow.'

'I'm glad. You know, Catherine, as an only child my situation was much the same as yours as I was growing up. I'm no Puritan—far from it. I loved all the pleasures in life—music, dancing—indeed, what young girl did not? Edward was much older than me and a hard man to love. And then I met Thomas. The attraction was there for both of us from the start. I didn't discourage his marriage to you when Edward suggested it. I couldn't marry him myself, so to keep Thomas near I agreed to it. It was wrong of me, I know that now, and you have suffered because of it. I resented you for having Thomas when I was as much to blame as your father for encouraging the match.'

'It's in the past, Blanche, and so much has changed.'

'What a mess it all is. You have changed, Catherine. Who would have thought that the girl who left here six years ago to live at Carlton Bray would return as a strong and independent woman?'

Catherine crossed to the door. 'The war has produced many women like me. Whether petitioning, defending castles or fighting alongside their husbands—a variety of activities of which none are passive—they all have a story to tell. I am no exception, Blanche. I did what I had to do. I'll leave you to finish what you're doing and have the coach made ready.'

Catherine saw Blanche and James into the coach. She was glad Jenny was going with them. Wherever Blanche was going she wouldn't be alone.

'Just a moment, Catherine,' Blanche said, leaning out of the half-open door.

'What is it, Blanche? Is there something you have forgotten?'

'I've thought long and hard about this and I think there is something you should know. When you next see your father, ask him about Thomas. Get him to tell you the manner of his death—the true manner of his death.'

Catherine stared at her, a cold shiver slithering down her spine. 'What are you saying?'

'You must ask Edward. If he doesn't tell you—then ask John.'

On that note she told the driver to move on. Catherine stood and watched the coach disappear down the drive. It was with reluctance she went back into the house. Whatever it was that her father and John knew and had decided not to tell her she could not begin to imagine, but that it was something sinister, something bad, she was certain of.

It was a long time after Blanche had left that Catherine plucked up the courage to confront her father. The bedchamber was warm, the steady light given out by the candles about the room throwing their glow on the large, canopied bed. Catherine eyed her father thoughtfully. He was huddled in shawls and coughing. His skin was waxen, his cheeks sunken, his breathing stertorous. He had changed so much in the short time she had been at Oakdene, caused by illness and twisted by griefs and bitterness, allowing no one to come too close to him. He had been asleep, but woke when she approached the bed. She stared down at him, fearing what he might disclose and tension weighing heavy on her spirit.

'Has she gone?' he asked, his voice a rasping wheeze.

'If you mean Blanche, then, yes, she's left. Have you any idea where she might have gone because she wouldn't tell me?'

'No. She can go to the devil for all I care.'

'Then I can only hope she has suitable lodgings for the sake of the child.'

'Aye,' he grumbled. 'Thomas Stratton's boy.'

She cleared her throat, moving closer to the bed. A cold sweat was breaking out on her brow. She didn't want to ask the question, but she knew she must. 'Father, tell me what happened to Thomas—the manner of his death.'

His eyes met hers in a sudden sharp, questioning regard and she quailed inside.

'Blanche has been talking, has she? I might have known she would.'

'Tell me. I want to know the truth. Is it so terrible?'

'He committed high treason. The sentence for that is death. It's the law.'

His mouth sat in a bitter line. Fear struck her for what would come next, a fear so profound that she became as cold as death. 'I see. What happened?'

'He was hanged.'

Catherine's heart stopped for a ghastly moment. The words hung in the air between them. Paralysed by his revelation, she felt the blood drain from her face. 'I see. That is indeed terrible. On whose orders?'

'Mine,' he said, raising his voice to such a high pitch that Catherine stepped away. 'I issued the order—me—and others.' He smiled, a grim, humourless smile. 'Thomas Stratton got what he deserved.'

In a blinding flash Catherine understood that her father's monstrous pride would wreak unspeakable revenge on Thomas for his crime against him, that of taking his wife—the charge of treason was all the excuse he needed. There was a pain inside her, writhing and living and ugly.

'How could you do that? Yes, he and Blanche were lovers, but did it not occur to you that he was also my husband? Or didn't it matter? Didn't *I* matter?'

'Thomas was executed for crimes against the country. It was the law.'

Catherine searched that hard face for some sign that he felt something for her, anything, but there was nothing. Bile rose in her throat as she realised that she didn't know her father at all. He was not one for regrets or introspection, and he felt entirely justified for his actions where Thomas was concerned.

'You should have told me. How could you keep this from me? How could you? I had a right to know how my husband died.' Unable to stay and look at the man who was the instigator of all her misery, she turned from him. At the door she paused and looked back. 'Tell me one thing. Did John know about Thomas?'

'John? Yes, he was there.'

For the rest of her life Catherine would remember that moment when the bottom dropped out of her world. Desperately hurt and angry at this final betrayal, she left him and returned to her own room. She felt hot, blazingly, ragingly hot and physically sick as she thought about what her father had told her. Each of his words had been like a blow to her head. Thomas's death and leaving Carlton Bray had meant a fresh start and no reminders of the past—if the past could ever be forgotten, for did it not always lie dormant, like a sleeping wild and hostile beast, waiting to spring up and sink its teeth into a defenceless heart?

The walls of her castle had proved to be made of paper. She had felt the first cold draughts blowing through them when Blanche had told her to ask her father about Thomas's death and she had felt the walls tremble and the wind howl strong when her father had told her the truth. Then they had collapsed around her feet.

Existing in the wreckage of her dream for a better life, she realised, beneath everything she had learned, just how much she actually loved John, but now the security that she had found with him was gone. Deep down she was furious at the injustice done to her—first her father for forcing her into a loveless marriage, then Thomas for discarding her as if she were something offensive, and now John. How could she trust him after this? It had been a mistake to trust him in the first place. The biggest mistake of all was that she had allowed him—wanted him—to make love to her and that was the most painful part.

Why did everyone she had ever known have to let her down? Her large eyes were wide with an effort to hold back the tears of angry despair. All that had been beautiful and exciting when John had left her that morning now lay in a heap of ashes at her feet.

Chapter Nine

After four days had passed and nothing was heard of Blanche, Catherine became so concerned that something might have happened to her that, with no one to turn to for advice, she decided to travel to Windsor to see John. Knowing what she did and unable to forgive him for the part he had played in Thomas's death, she would have preferred not to, but there was no one else she could turn to.

Leaving early and taking the coach in which she had travelled from Carlton Bray, with one of the grooms up front, she was relieved when she eventually saw the ramparts and turrets of Windsor Castle. It was being used not only as a Parliamentary garrison, but also as a prison, holding many Royalists. The majestic pile towered over the great park and meadows, the town stretching along the hill on which the castle was built.

After passing through the Castle Gate and undergoing the inspection of the guards, they entered the castle grounds. It was like a bustling town within the massive walls, with a patchwork of half-timbered houses and buildings in the Lower Ward. It lacked the uniformity of the Upper Ward of the castle, which housed the royal apartments used by kings and queens through the ages, but, with a diversity of buildings around it, the dazzling, magnificent St George's Chapel, the final resting place of monarchs and knights of England past, dominated the enclosure.

As she stepped down from the coach a soldier approached her and asked who she was looking for.

'I wish to see Colonel Stratton. I believe he is here.'

He nodded. 'Wait here. I'll see if I can find him.'

She waited, watching everyone go about their business, glad that she didn't draw attention to herself. And then John appeared. Ever since their night together she had not been able to put him out of her thoughts. Her mind was filled with images of him as he had been when they had parted after their search for James. Seeing him now, she cast them away, turning her thoughts back to her present predicament, and cringed inside at the thought of the outcome. He looked relaxed. He was laughing, calling something over his shoulder to a gentleman he passed. When he saw her he stopped. Their eyes met and locked for a moment, John's opening wider and wider, experiencing astonishment and incredulity and finally pleasure, before brusquely recollecting himself.

'Catherine! What are you doing here? Have you ridden here unaccompanied?'

'No. I travelled in the coach.'

'It's good to see you, but what brings you to Windsor? Come. We can't talk here.'

He led her to a room occupied by several gentlemen. Her arrival created a stir and a few ribald comments.

John cast a baleful eye over them and they made their excuses and left. They were alone at last.

'Well? Why are you here?'

'Two reasons.' Her voice was calm, much too calm and carefully modulated.

'Has something happened? Is it Edward?'

'No.'

'Why do you look at me like that?'

'My compliments, John,' she emphasised contemptuously, going straight to the attack, 'on your duplicity and your deceit.' When his face hardened she nodded. 'It would appear our relationship began on a lie. Yes, John. I accuse you of having deceived me, of telling me that Thomas had died from wounds sustained at some time or other, when all the time he had been charged with treason, sentenced to death and hanged.'

Completely taken off guard by her attack, John stared at her, speechless. 'Who told you of this?'

'My father. And please don't deny that you know about it because you were there, apparently. You had no right to keep the truth from me. There was no love between us, but I had a right to know how my husband died. Why did you keep a matter of such magnitude from me? Why did you lie to me?' she demanded.

'I did not lie. You did not ask and I thought you

would be better off not knowing. It was not an honourable way to die. I was trying to protect you.'

'I would like to have been the one to decide that—and I did not need protecting.'

'It was not by my hand that Thomas was executed. You cannot put the blame on my shoulders for events that happened that day.'

'No? You were there. You could have tried to stop it happening. You could have told me. I wanted the truth.'

As indignant as she was, John's entire body tensed and his jaw clenched so tightly that a muscle began to throb in his cheek. His look was cold and dispassionate, and completely in control. 'I can see my concern for your welfare has displeased you, Catherine. It was not my intention. Understandably you are distraught.'

'Your deception over the matter distressed and angered me almost beyond bearing—justifiably so. When we went to see Thomas's lawyer, I remember you having a private word with him before proceedings began. What did you say to him, John? Did you ask him not to mention the manner of Thomas's death lest it upset me?' The cold, silent look he gave her confirmed what she had suspected. 'How dare you do that? How could you? How precious little I have known. I feel as if I've struggled through a battlefield of lies and evasions. You and my father are as bad as each other. You were there, you saw what my father was doing, yet you did nothing to prevent it.'

'I couldn't.' His voice was chilling, with all the deadly calm of approaching peril. He moved closer, his eyes hard and compelling, holding hers so that she was unable to look away. 'With so little knowledge about what happened, you are too quick to judge. Neither I nor your father are the monsters you imagine us to be. Thomas was a spy, Catherine. He carried letters to and from the King on the Isle of Wight, to the young Charles in the Netherlands, or to France and over the border to the Scots—such was his loyalty to the cause. He was captured in Newcastle when he crossed over the border from Scotland. There is a death sentence for spying.'

'I didn't know he was a spy. I suppose I should have known there was more to it when he didn't come home. And of course my father couldn't wait to carry out the death sentence. He made good of the opportunity. Knowing what he did, I have no doubt he would have been happy to put the noose around his neck himself in order to exact his vengeance for his affair with Blanche and to be rid of him.'

'What is this, Catherine? Can't you bring yourself to admit that Thomas's actions were indefensible?'

'It affected me deeply when I discovered the truth about him—and the manner of his death. I do not condone his actions and, despite the fact that he preferred life on the battlefield to that of domesticity with his wife, I do not disapprove of them either since he was doing what he thought was right, what he went to war for.'

'He was a traitor.'

'So he deserved to hang?'

'I didn't say that.'

'You didn't have to.'

'It was war, Catherine, in all its brutality. It was about setting an example.'

'Yes, the country was at war. It was up to each man's conscience to decide whether take up arms for the King or Parliament, but I would not have wished him to die at the end of a rope. Thomas and I had our differences, you know that, but his loyalty to the King was never in doubt. Whatever happened the King must win. When it came to his own life it mattered very little. He was sincere and true—a Royalist—a peer of the realm,' she said vehemently, 'and no matter what crime he was guilty of he should have been brought to London to stand trial. If found guilty, then he should have been beheaded like a peer, not hanged. He should at the very least have died with dignity.'

'I deeply regret that I concealed the manner of Thomas's death, but I saw no reason to divulge it. I am sorry—'

'For what? Being party to Thomas's execution? Breaking my trust in you?'

'I should have told you. I realise that now. But Thomas is dead and bears no relevance to the future.'

'Have you told Blanche that? If not, then perhaps you should.'

'Blanche knows what happened to Thomas.'

'And their son? That child will find out one day about his father. And you—you were there.'

'To my everlasting regret I—'

'Please, John, spare me your excuses.'

John's eyes became locked on hers. 'I give no excuses. I deeply regret what happened to Thomas,' he said, his voice clipped, harsh, hiding the amazing depth of hurt that assailed his heart.

'Unlike my father. Were you influenced by my father, allowing your respect for him to cloud your mind to the true nature of his character, to the wickedness he carried in his heart for Thomas?'

'And you judge me with nothing more than this?'

'Yes, I do,' she answered in defiance of his challenge.

'Then I am sorry to disappoint you. Your accusations are unfounded. I had nothing whatsoever to do with Thomas's execution. You must take my word for that. It is clear to me that a seed that has been planted in your mind has blown out of all proportion. Your mind is made up. You clearly have little regard for my feelings towards you and you are more likely to listen to other people's words than mine.'

Catherine was shocked and full of bitterness and anger at his reaction, the sudden fury in his eyes, the tightening of his jaw and the lash of harshness in his words.

'But hear this,' he went on. 'I am not guilty of deceit. I simply did not tell you about Thomas because it was not for me to do so.'

She continued to look at him coldly. 'The implications of what I have learned about my father and your involvement in Thomas's terrible death I cannot begin to contemplate at this moment, or what it will mean to my future. Neither of you has anything to be proud of where Thomas was concerned. And now you must excuse me. I have other important matters to attend to.'

In stunned silence John watched her go. He stared at the doorway through which she had disappeared. The room was suddenly larger, somehow emptier. Recollecting himself, he strode after her. He couldn't let her go like this.

'Catherine, wait.'

Hearing his voice, she stopped, turned and waited for him to reach her.

The force of personality that burned in her eyes gave John an insight into the woman who had defended Carlton Bray Castle against Parliamentary patrols. She must have looked as she did now, with her solid will and defiance in every line of her body. She looked magnificent and a flood of admiration he was unable to prevent washed over him. But what she had said smote his heart and he turned his head away, unable to meet her direct gaze, to look upon the hatred she possessed for her father mirrored in their depths. He understood completely the reason for her anger. Not only did she feel abandoned by Thomas, she also felt betrayed by her father and himself.

She had come to London not knowing what to expect from her father. She had been young and naive enough, a willing victim ready to fall prey to the attention he might lavish on her after years of neglect.

Yet deep inside her heart she had always known the truth, but had refused to acknowledge it, knowing that, on doing so, the pain would be intolerable. Catherine was completely justified to feel as she did.

'You said there were two things that had brought you to Windsor. What was the other?'

'Yes—I forgot. It's Blanche. She left several days ago with James and his nurse. I'm concerned about them. She took the coach and intended to send it back when she was settled. I've heard nothing and I'm worried about her. I wondered if you might be able to throw some light on where she might have gone.'

'Yes, as a matter of fact I can. She came to me for help. She told me Edward had turned her out. Her and James. I sent her to Sussex—to stay with my mother.'

Catherine stared at him, incredulous. 'Why did you do that?'

'The child is a Stratton. As head of the family I have a duty of care to Thomas's son.'

'After being party to his death?' Shaking her head in anger and dismay, she turned from him. 'And no one thought to tell me where they were.'

'My time has been taken up with military matters, Catherine. Blanche told me she would inform you of her plans. Catherine, I—'

She turned back to him, a fierce light in her eyes. 'No,' she said, holding out her hand to keep him at bay. 'Leave it, John. I'm in no mood for further conversation. Whatever was between us is over. It should never have happened. You've spoilt everything. I valued your friendship above all others, but when friends become lovers that friendship suffers—as ours has done. I cannot forgive you your betrayal. I believe you are to go down to Sussex in a day or so. What can I say except that I hope you all have a happy Christmas?'

John watched her go in silence, his warrior instincts stirred by the depth of his passion for her, his desire to possess and protect her now stronger than ever. For the moment he must accept temporary defeat. But later he would find a way to make her listen. He watched her stalk back to her coach, defiance clear in the erect spine and the proud head held high. He would have gone after her and argued with her, but his short experience with Catherine Stratton had taught him to recognise intractable stubbornness when he saw it. By the time she reached Oakdene, hopefully she would have calmed down. He would make a point of going to see her before the day was out. It was imperative that she heard the truth about what had happened to Thomas. Sadly, she had a twisted view of the truth and for him to be absolved from blame and her own sanity she had to know what had occurred.

John didn't get the chance to go to Oakdene that day. No sooner had Catherine left him than word reached him at Windsor that the King had been removed from the Isle of Wight and was on his way to London. He had been summoned to join the large escort.

Travelling away from Windsor, Catherine felt dead inside and she wondered if the pain in her heart would ever go away. Her mind ranged through the evocative memories left over from the days she had spent with John. Though sorely lacking experience in the realm of desire, instinct assured her the wanton yearnings gnawing at the pit of her being were nothing less than cravings that John had elicited with his mere presence. The night they had spent making love, he had known full well what he was doing to her and that he was capable of annihilating her will, her mind and her soul, and now she would hunger for ever for that same devastating ecstasy. But she would not allow herself to become caught up in a romantic dream. Her emotions were torn asunder and she could find no solace in the depths of her thoughts.

She looked down the long, lonely corridor of her future. It was worse than tears would have been, that silent acceptance, thinking of the man she had trusted so completely and who just as completely had deceived her. She must force herself to believe that their embraces had never happened, that everything was the same as before. But she knew that the despairing pain she felt would always be there. It might dull with the years, but it would never leave her and she would grieve for his loss as though he were dead.

Suddenly she was overwhelmed with bitterness and frustration because so many men had taken control over her life. Staunchly she decided at that moment that it was time she took charge of her own life and started thinking for herself. The idea of going to Wilsden Manor appealed to her more than ever—though it would mean selling Oakdene to do so. Only there would she find the peace and solace she craved.

When she arrived back at Oakdene, Mrs Coleman was in the kitchen supervising the cooking for the evening meal. Hearing Catherine, she hurried out.

'Oh, my lady, thank goodness you're back.'

'Why, what is it, Mrs Coleman? Has something happened?'

'It has. It's the master. He's taken a turn for the worse—another seizure—a bad one this time. I've taken the liberty of sending for the doctor. He should be here any time.'

A coldness settled over Catherine like a suffocating shroud. 'Is—is he conscious?'

Mrs Coleman shook her head. 'I'm afraid not.'

'Thank you. Is there anyone with him?'

'One of the servants.'

'I'll go and sit with him until the doctor arrives.'

Entering her father's room, she thanked the young maid and waited until she was out the door before she moved to the bed. Her father was shrunk against the pillows. His face was white, one side of his mouth pulled down. His life was drawing to a close. There was nothing she could do other that sit beside the bed and wait and look at his paralysed face. His eyes were closed, his breathing shallow, each breath more difficult than the last, and she knew he was slipping away.

The doctor came and went. There was nothing more he could do. It was just a matter of time—perhaps a day or just hours. Catherine continued her silent vigil, reluctant to analyse how she felt just then. That would come later. The shadows of evening darkened the room. Eventually, exhaustion claimed her and she dozed in her chair. Her father's breathing grew more laboured, but he did not wake. His face was transparent, his eyes sunken. Catherine sat still and watched as he passed away. She shed no tears at his passing and felt no pain at his loss, only a strange sense of release. Getting to her feet, she went to inform Mrs Coleman.

Catherine wrote to Blanche informing her of her father's death. After all that had transpired before she left Oakdene, she didn't expect her to return, but she invited her to do so if she so wished. She sent a letter to army headquarters at Windsor for John, but she imagined he'd left for Sussex. If so, Blanche would give him the news.

The arrangements were made for her father's burial in the local churchyard, where her mother had been laid to rest. She carried it out quietly and efficiently. People from the surrounding neighbourhood and acquaintances came to pay their respects and offer condolences. It was the second funeral she had organised in six weeks and she was vastly relieved to get it over with.

To take her mind off everything she busied herself with sorting out her father's papers and legal matters. His lawyer came to read the will and finally it was over. It was as she expected. Everything had been left to her—the house and his wealth. There was nothing for Blanche. Bitterness at his cruelty ate at her. Blanche and Catherine might have had their differences, but Blanche had been his wife for eight years. She had deserved something.

The pain of the past days grew worse in Catherine, filling the days ahead with an inner despair which she strove to hide, burying it deep inside her. She had not seen John or heard from him since the day at Windsor, but she knew, no matter how hard she tried to think otherwise, that since then nothing had been the same. The pleasure and the intensity she had experienced on John's last night at Oakdene were now too painful to think about.

But they would not go away. She was haunted, too, by the memory of the passionate night she had spent in his arms and the response of her body. A look from him could steal her breath and rob her mind of all reason. Her mind became a battleground of conflicting emotions. She wanted him, but a stubborn part of her held back. Still the memories gave her no peace. She was plagued by the whispering echoes of the rapture she had tasted and his kiss and the passion which his touch had ignited. There was no denying the pleasure John could give a woman. If that was all a woman wanted, then he had no equal. But her ideals had changed. Now she needed more than a frenzied affair that engaged her body and mind, but not her heart.

News came to Oakdene that the captive King Charles had arrived at Windsor Castle just two days before Christmas. He had returned to the capital, not in honour, as he desired, but as a prisoner. He stubbornly refused to negotiate with Parliament or the army, so here he would remain while his opponents discussed his fate. There was encouragement from the people who cheered him as he passed towards Windsor, some even crying out for God to bless him.

There was no good cheer at Oakdene that Christmas. It was a house in mourning, but Catherine did not mourn her father. Oakdene was no longer the home she had known as a child and never would be again. Her father's presence, even though he no longer inhabited the house, could be felt in every room. She had the strange sensation that she was being watched by a silent shadow that chilled the air like winter ice. Depression settled round her shoulders like a leaden cloak.

When Thomas had died she had sought freedom from the constraints of her sex. Now, after her experience with John, she found herself tied by her own imagination. She would give anything to escape the agonising heartache tearing her apart. She wanted to love and to be loved, to experience the impossible dream of romance. But then she laughed and mocked herself for the absurdity of it all. Better for her peace of mind if she stopped dreaming and fantasising about such things.

It was early in January when a visitor rode to up to the house. The hour was late and she was about to prepare for bed. Catherine heard the knocking at the door. When no one answered, the urgent knocking came again. Eventually one of the servants opened it and the caller was admitted.

Catherine went out to see who it was and was surprised to see John removing his cloak and hat. Mechanically going through the motions of existence and survival, she was unsure how to receive him after their last angry encounter. The memory of their last meeting was still fresh in her mind and, as far as she was concerned, nothing had changed. They stood and looked at each other. Catherine's face was pale but composed, her emotions well in hand.

'I had to come and see you. I can understand why you may be reluctant to see me, but there is too much that has been left unsaid between us.'

'You mean there is more?'

'Much more. Now if you would be so kind as to listen, I think we should retire to the parlour.'

Without a word Catherine went back inside. John followed and closed the door.

The parlour suddenly seemed too small for John's towering height as he stood facing her. His close presence emanated a sense of controlled power straining beneath the surface. She stood motionless, acutely aware of her nerves stretching to breaking point. Just when she thought that she would not be affected by him he appeared and all her carefully tended illusions were dashed. No matter how hard she tried to appear calm and in control of her emotions, her heart set up its familiar, wild beating as she looked into his face. The lines were heavy about his mouth and cheeks and there were signs of strain and fatigue under his blue eyes. He gave her a long, thoughtful stare. The silence between them seemed to stretch into infinity.

'I've ridden from London,' he said at length. 'I have to get to Windsor, but I wanted to see you.' He studied her, relaxing slightly as his gaze caressed her lovely features. She did not seem herself, which he put down to her father's death. 'I heard about your father. I've come to offer my condolences. I'm sorry I wasn't here and that you had to deal with it alone.'

'Yes.' She moved towards him, but then she checked herself and drew back, putting distance between them. 'He had another seizure that proved fatal.' She saw sympathy in his eyes and she remembered the John Stratton she had known, cool and self-confident. Now he stood before her, dignified in the face of death.

'And you, Catherine? How are you?'

'As you see. I am well.'

'If there is any way I can be of help, you only have to ask.'

'Thank you. I do not think there is anything you—anyone—can do. Will you have some wine or something else, perhaps?'

'No—I won't. Time is of the essence.'

She did not press the issue. 'You have been down to Sussex for Christmas?'

His gaze searched hers, but their depths were deliberately shuttered. 'No. It was what I intended, but military duties meant I had to remain here. The King was on the move from the Isle of Wight and I was called on to go to Hampshire to assist in escorting him to Windsor. I've been gone over two weeks and only recently returned. I came as soon as I read your message.'

'I see. That's a shame. You will have been missed by your family.'

'They'll understand. My youngest brother and his family were to be there. They have young children which will have been good for James. I understand he's had very little interaction with other children.'

'He was a lonely little boy living here. I'm sure Blanche will have been glad for him to have the company of other children. I didn't expect her to come back for the funeral. I do not blame her for not doing so. What is to be done with the King? Is he to remain at Windsor?'

'For the time being. He has always been happy there. Negotiations have come to nothing and the Commons have voted that he be summoned for public trial on the grounds that he has levied war against Parliament and the Kingdom.'

'When will it be?'

'The twentieth of January.'

'So soon? How has he taken this blow from fate?'

'With quiet dignity. He is ready.'

'I cannot help thinking that it is a tragic thing that a King must stand trial for his life.'

'And it will be his life that they demand. There are many supporters of Parliament and the Army that shrink from either the trial itself or the consequences. Many eminent and respected lawyers have retired from the capital. The King is convinced that afterwards his son Charles will be King of England.'

'You imply that he has already been tried and condemned.'

He nodded, his expression grave. 'I know how this sorry business must end.'

They fell silent, each lost in their own thoughts as the fire crackled and snapped when it caught the wood Catherine had fed into its glowing heart earlier.

John's gaze settled on his companion. 'Enough talk of King Charles, Catherine, for where he is concerned what will be will be with not a thing you or I can do about it. I have come to see you. I was concerned following our meeting at Windsor. You were clearly upset by what your father had told you. I fully intended on coming to see you until I was called away.'

'Why, John? Why did you want to see me? I thought everything had been said between us.'

'Not everything. Understandably, in the circumstances you were already hurt and suffering and I compounded that by keeping the tragic circumstances of Thomas's death from you. If I had wanted to destroy your self-esteem, I could not have made a better job of it. Your father did not tell you all of what happened in Newcastle. Indeed, he did not tell you the whole truth. I want you to hear my account of what happened.'

Catherine nodded and indicated that they should sit. 'Then you'd better tell me,' she said as they took a seat on either side of the hearth where the glowing embers of the fire provided a welcome warmth against the chill of the winter's day. 'If there is more, I would be glad to hear it—and no half-truths. I want to know all of it.'

'I will tell you. When you came to me at Windsor you were angry and upset—and rightly so. But I am not inhuman. You were correct in saying that Thomas deserved better. By the time I reached Newcastle where Thomas and other Royalists were captured, it was already too late. The sentence had been carried out. You should also know that, despite what he told you, your father was not to blame. He wanted him taken to London to stand trial, but tempers were running high and no one would listen. There was criticism in many quarters at the handling of the brief trial and the passing of the sentence. You were correct when you said that as a peer of the realm—whatever his crime—he should not be treated like a commoner. That has ever been our English precedent. Thomas himself protested—he had not really dared hope for pardon, but he had hoped to die with dignity.'

'Did he deserve to die at all?'

'That is no easy question to answer. Thomas carried letters for the King. He knew there was a price on his head. In short, Catherine, he was no saint.'

'Were any of the men who took up arms on either side?' she said quietly.

'No. But most of them followed their beliefs. Thomas knew what he was doing, that it was dangerous and that he faced the death penalty if caught. After the battle at Marston Moor, even the King's most ardent supporters were reluctant to carry on fighting for what they could rightly see as a doomed cause and that the price for supporting the losing side would be enormous. Few were willing to risk what they had left.'

'But not Thomas.'

'No. He continued to seek out support for the King among his old friends, but even had he succeeded there was little of what was needed—arms and money.' He sighed deeply. 'Thomas and I may have fought on opposing sides, but he was a brave man, Catherine. Never doubt that. Young James must be told of the part his father played during the conflict and be proud.'

'And my father?'

'Whatever you have been told, he did not pass the final judgement on Thomas. He was extremely ill and anxious to get back to Oakdene. You may be surprised to learn that he suffered not only from ill health, but also a deep regret when the sentence was carried out. Yes, he wanted to wreak his vengeance for Thomas's crime against himself, but that was personal, a separate matter that had nothing to do with the war.'

'My father was so bitter and angry, driven by wrongdoings against him. I think the pain caused by his illness and what had been done to him had crippled his mind and impaired his judgement and pushed him to extremes. But what of you, John? Where were you while all this was happening?'

'I had duties elsewhere in the north. Where Blanche is concerned, I have given the matter much thought.

The best thing for all concerned is that she takes James to Carlton Bray. It is his rightful place. It is what Thomas would have wanted. James will be told of his father. A boy should hear about his father's courage—about loyalties and convictions, whatever they may be—and be proud. Blanche also has to be taken care of. For the present they are being well taken care of in Sussex. When the time is right I will go with them to Carlton Bray. Do you approve of that?'

'It is only right that you should be concerned for James and his well-being. Carlton Bray is no longer my concern, but I do think it would be appropriate for James to grow up there. Have you discussed this with Blanche?'

'No. I haven't been down to Sussex as yet, but I cannot imagine she will object.'

'No matter how hard you try, John, you cannot legitimise James.'

'I realise that.'

'Unless…' She faltered, biting her lips, reluctant to make a suggestion that was abhorrent to her and wishing she hadn't started.

Frowning, John glanced across at her. 'Unless? Unless what, Catherine?'

'I am sure you have considered all possibilities for Blanche and I would not presume to suggest otherwise. I think you will deal with the situation very well without my input.'

'Anything you say, Catherine, I will consider seriously. Tell me what you've thought of—and are unwilling to voice should I find it not to my liking.'

'That's just it, John, you might like it very well. I was about to say that you could marry Blanche and adopt James at a later date. Blanche is a widow—an attractive widow. She is free to marry again sooner than you expected.'

He looked at her closely, studying her face, but unable to see past her cool façade. 'Do you think that would be appropriate, Catherine?'

Shaking her head, she leaned forward and picked up a log from the hearth, setting it on the fire and making a point of keeping her face low. 'How would I know? I am sure you will do what is right where Blanche is concerned.' If she was able to make herself accept it, to believe it, to be unconcerned that he might very well make Blanche a part of his life, she would have to wallow in the pain of it—like salt in an open wound that was agonising, but healing—and then she must learn to suffocate all her feelings for him, not think of him.

'Catherine,' he said, his tone soft, 'I have no wish to marry Blanche. There are other ways of securing Carlton Bray for James. Now I am back at Windsor I will make the time to go and see Thomas's lawyer— to get some advice on the legal side of things. I would like to have it made over to James—that's something I will look into in the future. It would not bode well at present, James's father being a Royalist. Before the war Carlton Bray was a splendid estate—and it will be again, I am certain of it. It has been too long without a master.'

The silence that followed was long and heavy. The firelight cast shadows over his handsome face, making his expression stern. 'It is not a criticism, Catherine. You could not have done more, but it would be advantageous to me to have someone living there and who better than Blanche and Thomas's son. You would probably say that Blanche's fate is nothing to do with you or me, but you would be wrong. Do not shut yourself off from her. She is hurting more than she lets anyone know. Thomas's death preys heavy on her mind. She loved him with her heart and soul and, as a mother, she wants the best for his son.'

'Yes, I am sure she did love Thomas, but she did not set eyes on him again after he left her in York almost four years ago, which was when she returned to Oakdene. And please don't tell me it was the war that halted communication between them because I won't believe it. I believe the reason she didn't inform him of James's birth is because she knew she couldn't have Thomas and tried to pass the child off as my father's to legitimise him, but he was having none of it.'

'This is nothing to do with war and divided loyalties, Catherine. This is about family and doing what is right. I will have to go down to Sussex soon to see her, I have to put things right. If I didn't do this, I would have contempt for myself.'

'Then you must do what you have to do, John.' She got to her feet. 'You said you were in a hurry. Don't let me keep you. It's dark and the road back to Windsor is not the best.'

Getting up, John faced her, studying her, his eyes devoid of emotion. For the first time she had been close to him and he'd let his guard down and revealed the man behind the title and the stern façade, but now, standing before her, he was a stranger, keeping his emotions and thoughts in check. She desperately wanted to know how to reach him, but could think of no way.

'I'm sorry you have to go. Please take care.'

'I don't understand you, Catherine. I can still feel your coldness. Our friendship is special. You are special to me and I hate to quarrel over this. Have you so little faith in me?' Even as he spoke he could feel her tension, tinged with sadness.

All the colour left Catherine's face. 'I understand what you are saying, but it changes nothing. Yes, our friendship is special,' she said heavily. 'It means a great deal to me and I value it greatly. But what happened between us will not be repeated.'

Suddenly there was such intensity in his gaze that Catherine felt her heartbeat quicken.

'Why? Afraid?' he enquired.

There was a challenge in his voice, in his eyes as well. She looked at him for a long moment before replying, 'No, John. I'm not afraid.'

'Then tell me that you haven't thought about me every day since we met—that you haven't dwelt on that one night when we became lovers. You cannot pretend it never happened, or that you weren't a willing partner.'

'Damn you, John. You know I can't do that.'

'I came here tonight to put things right between us. I hoped I had done that.'

She sighed. 'Thank you for explaining everything to me. I do appreciate you coming.'

Without saying more he turned on his heel and walked to the door, halting to look back once more to where she stood motionless. The firelight gave her deep golden hair a halo of light. He hesitated, appeared to change his mind and calmly, deliberately, retraced his steps until he was standing before her. Catherine's immediate action was to retreat, but before she could do so she found herself held by his arm about her waist, breathing in the sweet scent of her. He took her mouth with his own. It was possessive, thorough, a branding of ownership, and then he released her as quickly as he had taken her in his arms,

'Do you really think you can dismiss me so easily? I spoke of friendship, but it is more than that. Understand me when I say I love you, Catherine. I will not give you up—nor will I let you give me up. You have been the victim of a terrible misfortune. I can only apologise for any part I played in that. It was never my aim to humiliate or distress you.' He paused to register the moment of surprise and shock in her wide eyes at this unexpected declaration. 'You have my heart—the whole of it. There,' he said, stepping back. 'That will give you something to think about in the days ahead.'

He stood tall and motionless, continuing to watch her reaction with enigmatic eyes, awaiting her reply. He was so sure of her, Catherine thought, so sure that no woman with fire in her veins could refuse him. His words revealed to her the depth of hurt he was feeling. How could she have been so blind to it? He continued to hold her gaze, reminding her that here was a man of strong passions, who would want a full and loving relationship with the woman he chose to spend his life with, no matter what. And yet for her own peace of mind and to hold on to her sanity, she must ignore the ache in her heart as she saw his pain.

'I—I don't know what to say. I—I never expected...'

'Do you deliberately set out to stoke my anger—to provoke me? You clearly have a very low opinion of me and of my motives for trying to untangle this dilemma we find ourselves in.'

'We? No, John, it is not my dilemma. Since my father died I've given much thought to my future. Never have I been more certain of what course my life will take.'

'I see. Then perhaps I must finally accept that it is impossible for me to win your respect, much less your love.' There was no hiding the bitterness of his words. When she would have opened her mouth to reply, he placed a finger on her lips, silencing her. 'Don't say anything just now. I may not be able to come for some time. With the King at Windsor, there are people coming and going all the time—but I will be back. I promise you.'

She followed him out of the house, her eyes shadowed by pain. He took possession of her hand and raised it to his lips. She longed to respond to the pressure of his hand, to feel his mouth on hers setting her skin tingling and her blood on fire, but with no words that would ease her heart or his own, she stood aside as he mounted his horse.

'John.' About to ride off, he paused and looked down at her. 'Please try to understand why I acted as I did when my father told me about what happened in Newcastle. I—I am sorry I misjudged you—truly I am.'

Leaning down from the saddle, he took her arm and drew her close. 'I do understand, Catherine. We will speak very soon and, in the meantime, think about what I said. I love you—and that is something I have never said to any woman.' He pressed her upturned lips with his own, his kiss brief.'

Catherine watched him ride away, fighting against the impulse to call him back. Her thoughts were in a turmoil. She stood there until she could no longer hear the beat of his horse's hooves on the gravel drive. Her arms and her heart had never felt so empty.

Having no wish to dwell on her thoughts, she went to the library to find something to read that would occupy her mind. Idly perusing the many leather-bound volumes on the shelves, but unable to find a book that appealed to her present mood, she decided to abandon the idea.

What stood out in her mind above all else was that

he had told her that he loved her. She had not chosen to feel so deeply for him and did not know the exact moment it had happened. She forced herself to go over every detail of that one night of blissful passion she had spent in his arms. It was like a self-scourging, a deliberate act on her part to try to purge herself of the feelings she had for him, but it was impossible, and, she thought, she no longer wanted to.

John had been unprepared for the cool young woman who had received him. On his mission to assist in escorting the King to Windsor he had thought of Catherine constantly, wanting her with a passion that shocked him. For the first time in his life his emotions were slipping out of his control. In his mind's eye he had an image of her loveliness that had been displayed so temptingly when she had shared his bed, the way her hair had draped itself over his chest when she had lain in his arms. There was a sensual earthiness in her lovely face, a proud elegance to her high cheekbones and a delicate curve to her slender neck.

It seemed he had been denied her for ever. Every nerve in his body was aware of her sensuality. He remembered the softness of her body, her submission to his caresses as her glorious body has yielded to his. What had followed had been the most erotic and sexual experience of his life. With this in mind he refused to allow her to disappear from his life.

She had been hurt by Thomas's neglect and he knew she would never again bind herself to a man she did not love and who would not love her in return. John had never known that kind of love, nor had he sought it. But that was before he had met Catherine and she could never be a fleeting affair. Her body invited him with every graceful move, every look from her beautiful green eyes, every heart-stopping smile on her lovely lips.

But he could not ignore the shadow of guilt that touched his heart. Hers was indeed an unenviable position. When she had married Thomas she had been very young and a pawn in a vicious game of politics played out by her father and Thomas. She deserved better.

As the days passed in a haze of melancholy and heartache for Catherine, and she busied herself with the task of sorting out her father's possessions and packing them up to store in the attics, she forced herself to smother all thoughts and feelings for John. In her quiet moments her thoughts would turn to him. Even when sleep embraced her, she had no respite, for he filled her dreams.

She longed to see him, to feel his lips on her, the touch of his hands, his presence—to hear the sound of his voice. When she thought that he might not forgive her for doubting him and he might not come back, she was engulfed with a sense of loss and sadness. Was that the price she must pay for her wilfulness and pride?

Chapter Ten

It was the feeling of nausea that first alarmed her, its continuation making her feel thoroughly wretched. At first she thought she was sickening for something as she moped about the house and did her chores in a depressed state. But when it did not subside, the idea that there was every possibility that she was with child, was carrying John's child, hit her like some cold, unwelcome shockwave.

In her innocence and everything that had happened since their night together, she had barely considered the consequences. She had thought the failure of her monthly cycle was because she was upset. But now she knew differently. How stupid and naive she had been. She should have expected this from a man like John. Strong and full blooded, he had impregnated her with an ease she did not find surprising.

She knew a feeling of desperation. What could she do? In a few months, if she really was with child, everyone would know of it. What would she say? She was only recently widowed, but not so recent that she could tell the world that Thomas was the father. People would say that she was a wanton woman, a strumpet—unless she went to a retreat somewhere where she could hide away for the rest of her life. Or, she thought, hope beginning to stir in her, she could go to Wilsden Manor in Hereford. Faced with a situation she did not know how to deal with, the mere thought of going to the house her mother had bequeathed to her raised her spirits.

She did consider writing to John, informing him of her condition, but something stopped her doing this immediately. It was early days and she might be mistaken. She would write to him, telling him of her decision to leave and that she believed she was with child before she left for Wilsden, where she could put her life in order. Throughout the war she'd had so much to do, so many dependents at Carlton Bray who had relied on her to do the right thing, to keep them safe from marauding bands of soldiers on either side. And since coming to Oakdene she'd had her father to consider and the everyday running of the house, so she'd had no time for herself, no time to think about what she wanted to do with her life.

At some later date she would consider putting Oakdene House up for sale or rent it out. It wasn't a decision she would have to make at present. Having decided, there was nothing to be done but pack her belongings, inform Mrs Coleman of her destination, and instruct her to carry on running the house until further notice.

* * *

The King had been brought from Windsor to St James's the day before the trial. The next day he was taken in a closed sedan chair to Whitehall and thence, in his own barge, to Westminster. The weather was bitingly cold. Attired in her breeches and shrouded in a fur-lined cloak, a wide-brimmed hat on her head, Catherine went into the city, tired of the inactivity forced on her now she had put the house in order. She intended to see her father's lawyer to settle some of his affairs, which she had reason to regret and wish she'd left it for the time being since London was a heaving mass of people who had poured in to witness the trial. There were a large number of soldiers on the streets, keeping an eye on the crowds. Frost whitened the roofs and spires beyond the city walls and the smoke curling out of the chimneys was sluggish in the dull light of day.

Her business completed, she found herself among the spectators that thronged the river and banks to watch as the King's barge passed by. Dismounting and keeping firm hold of her horse, she stood among the crowd as people jostled with each other, the odour of unwashed bodies rank in the air. Some cheered, but the barge, closely followed and preceded by guards, was enclosed so no one could get a glimpse of the beleaguered monarch. Catherine felt the chill of the day, but the greater chill came from within as she stared at the barge.

Unable to see more when the crowd surged in front of her, she led her horse away, only to feel someone trying to pull the reins from her grasp. Catherine started in surprise, her blood running cold. Two men stood in her path. At first she did not heed them and made to pass them by, but they lunged at her horse, a fine specimen of horseflesh, with the intent of stealing it. The horse tossed its head and skittered sideways. Somehow Catherine managed to keep a firm hold on the reins. Another man with long greasy hair and ill-fitting grubby clothes jumped out and seized its bridle. She let out a cry as she struggled to keep hold of the reins.

The man gave a bitter laugh, his thin lips drawing back over blackening teeth. 'Let go if you know what's good for you,' he growled, grasping and twisting her arm and trying to prise her fingers off the reins. ''Tis a fine horse. 'Twill do me well.'

'Let go of my horse,' she cried, hoping and praying someone would take note of her plight and come to her aid.

With a coarse chuckle the man eyed her closely. 'Well, and just look at what we 'ave 'ere. A beauty if ever I saw one. Pity we can't take you along with the 'orse, but it'd be too troublesome.'

Frost hung in the air, making Catherine's breath steam. She did not feel the cold. She felt anger and there was a wildness in her eyes as she pushed her cloak back over one shoulder, revealing that she was dressed in man's attire. Seeing this, the man with the greasy hair relaxed a little, exhaling a breath, his eyes getting their fill.

'Well, now, what have we here—a lass dressed as a lad.'

When he reached out to take hold of her, she whirled around and planted her elbow in his soft gut. He staggered backwards, cursing loudly. His accomplice was too busy trying to hold on to the horse to go to his companion's aid. Mercifully, when the man she had lashed out at found his feet and would have taken hold of her, three soldiers rode up to them, one of them dismounting and pushing the thief to the ground. The thief, his eyes wide and fearful, looked up at the soldier, holding his belly where Catherine's elbow had connected.

'We weren't doin' any 'arm,' he gasped, shoving himself backwards on the ground and then scrambling to his feet.

'No?' one of the soldiers said, having drawn his sword and holding it in a threatening way in front of the thief. 'You were about to steal this young gentleman's horse. Away with you, both of you,' he said, 'before I find a soft place to stick my sword. Get on your way.'

His companion, seeing the soldiers bearing down on him, let go of Catherine's horse and bolted, to be quickly followed by his accomplice.

Catherine turned to thank the soldiers, only to be invaded by a nameless horror as she saw who stood there. It was John. His tall, broad-shouldered figure blocked the light and seemed to fill her whole vision. That was the moment she wanted the ground to open and swallow her up. The blood left her face and rushed to her heart, which seemed to have stopped beating. She tried to pull her broad-brimmed hat down over her face, but it was no good. He had recognised her. A mixture of puzzlement and anger crossed his face. Her eyes never left his, which were wide and savagely furious as he looked at her in murderous silence, his lips curling with anger as he absorbed the scene.

'You!' he gasped. 'What the hell are you doing here?'

With a wildly beating heart, she stammered, 'John... I...'

His temper threatening to explode on finding her in such a dangerous situation, he uttered, 'Wait here.' Turning from her, he went to his two companions. He spoke to them quietly and, after glancing in her direction with knowing, almost lecherous smiles, they rode away.

With a terrible dread Catherine waited in a state of jarring tension for the inevitable moment when John would turn his attention on her. Her trembling had finally ceased, but she kept playing the thief's terrible attack over and over in her mind, remembering the loathsome feel of his hands on her arm, and then her feeling of absolute relief when the soldiers had appeared. She would be forever grateful for their timely arrival and relieved that they had dealt with the situation quickly. But it must have been a shock to John's sensibilities to find her on the London streets being attacked by a couple of horse thieves. She was deeply concerned that she would receive the brunt of his anger.

His expression was of deep concern. 'Catherine—what the devil are you about? Have you no sense? Today is not the day you should have chosen to come into the city. It's madness.'

'I do realise that now.'

'I hope you have a good explanation for your conduct.'

'I had to come to see my father's lawyer. I never gave the King's trial a thought.'

'Clearly,' he snapped, taking the reins out of her hands to take hold of her horse. 'Haven't you the sense you were born with?'

Catherine glowered at him from beneath the wide brim of her hat. 'Yes, I have, John, and I won't be treated like some milksop who is likely to break in two at the slightest pressure.'

'I realised that the first time I met you. But you would be in great danger should things get out of hand—which could happen at the slightest provocation. I should have called on you before now, but throughout the days the King has been brought back to London I've been kept busy night and day with no time to spare. Now come with me and I'll escort you back to Oakdene.'

Catherine had no choice but to do as she was told since he had charge of her horse. He was clearly concerned for her and he had spoken the truth. She should have had more sense than to venture into the city today of all days.

They mounted their horses and rode out of the city. Only then did Catherine speak.

'You can leave me now. I'm sure you have more important matters that need your attention than escorting me back to Oakdene. I can make my own way home.' One look at his face told Catherine that he was still in a dangerous mood.

'I'm going with you. It's not safe for you to be out riding alone. Have you any idea what could have happened to you back there? You could have been seriously hurt—or worse—by your ill-considered actions. You could at least have had the sense to let a groom accompany you. These are troubled times, with people from all over England converging on London to witness the trial of the King. The next time you go riding, do not go unaccompanied. Do you understand, Catherine?'

Catherine's face flamed with indignation. 'Insist all you like, John, but I am capable of making my own decisions—and I prefer to ride home alone. I object most strongly to your—'

'I'm going with you, so don't argue. I want to make sure you arrive at Oakdene in one piece.'

Only a few hours before this tirade would have reduced Catherine to submission. But now it left her unmoved and angry. 'I am not one of your soldiers, John. I am not one or your subordinates, so please do not treat me as one. If you cannot speak to me in a civil manner, then I will take my leave of you now.'

On that note she pressed her knees into her horse's sides and urged it on, hearing him curse softly. During the struggle with her assailants her hair had slipped from the careless knot at the back of her neck. Now, from beneath her hat, it fell in gentle waves about her shoulders. In the grey light of day, she looked like a wild, tawny owl. Catherine knew John continued to follow her, but she did not look back.

It was dusk by the time they reached Oakdene. Catherine left her horse for the grooms to take care of and strode to the house, ignoring John, who dismounted and followed her to the door.

On entering the hall and seeing the baggage piled up ready to be strapped to the coach the following morning for her journey to Hereford, he stood still.

'What's this? Are you going somewhere, Catherine?'

A fervent glitter brightened Catherine's eyes. 'Yes. I've decided to go away—to leave Oakdene. I don't want to be here any more.'

'Where are you going?'

'Wilsden. I leave for Wilsden Manor tomorrow.'

John turned to face her in astonishment. 'Wilsden? You were just going to disappear? Did you not think to notify me? Did it not enter your head that I would be concerned, that I would want to know?'

'No, John. I know how busy you are at present.'

'How could you be so foolish? You must know that I want to be with you more than anyone.'

She said, 'I was not sure...'

'How could you think of going away?'

'I was going to write and let you know. Besides, I do not intend going for good—at least, I don't think so. I just thought some time to myself is what I need just now. Wilsden Manor seemed a good idea.'

'But that's miles away in Hereford. Do I have to point out the dangers for a woman travelling alone with thieves and cutthroats and all manner of undesirables lying in wait for a coach to pass by—not to mention the state of the roads at this time of year? An axle could break and you would find yourself in a ditch in the middle nowhere. Has that thought not entered that stubborn head of yours?'

'I am well aware of everything you have pointed out, John, which is why I shall take three of the grooms with me and do all my travelling by day. I am not as helpless as you appear to think.'

'With a pistol and a dagger in your belt I imagine you are confident you will survive any kind of attack,' he scoffed, 'but you are wrong.'

Catherine was about to respond with a scathing remark when she was aware of Mrs Coleman hovering across the hall.

'I'm sorry, my lady. I did not wish to intrude, but I heard raised voices and...'

'It's quite all right, Mrs Coleman. Please don't be concerned. His Lordship was just chastising me—most severely, I can tell you—for riding into the city without an escort. It had slipped my mind that today is the start of the King's trial and the city's positively heaving with humanity. Would you have some refreshment brought to the parlour—something warming? It's been a cold ride from the city.'

'I will—at once.' She scuttled away to do Catherine's bidding.

Catherine turned back to John, who was glaring at her with his hands on his hips. 'Well? Have you finished berating me? If not, then I insist that you leave. I'm in no mood for an argument. Otherwise you are welcome to stay and take some refreshment before you return to your duties.'

Without waiting for him to reply she strode into the parlour, relieved to find Mrs Coleman had drawn the heavy velvet curtains and that a roaring fire was blazing in the hearth. John followed and closed the door. Taking a seat to the side of the hearth, he stretched out his legs and rested his feet on the brass fender, his damp boots beginning to steam with the direct heat. Catherine looked at him, amazed that he could look so disgustingly relaxed after berating her so harshly.

With her arms crossed tightly over her breasts, she glowered at him. 'Since you have made yourself so comfortable, my lord, I assume that means you have finished chastising me.'

'I did not agree to stay to trade insults with you, Catherine, but it's your own fault that I was so severe with you.' Turning his head to look at her, he gave her a wicked smile, an indication that his mood was softening.

'Oh, really? I cannot wait to hear the reasoning behind that statement.'

'You provoke me.'

'You provoke me as well and I will not speak aloud all the names I have called you in my mind since leaving the city. No doubt my brush with those thieves provided entertainment for your companions—and you.'

'It certainly created some amusement—despite my shock on finding you among the crowd hoping for a glimpse of His Majesty.'

'I imagine you were. I trust your appetite for sadistic amusement has been satisfied.'

'For the present,' he replied, making himself more comfortable in the chair.

Mrs Coleman entered bearing a tray of cold meats and bread and cheese and warm muffins, a speciality of hers, placing it on a table in the middle of where they sat, so it could be reached easily. When she left Catherine divided the food onto plates and handed one to John, before pouring warm spiced wine into two goblets.

The wine soothed Catherine's frazzled nerves. They ate slowly, speaking little—presenting a tableau of domestic bliss, Catherine thought, to anyone looking on. Little would they imagine the turmoil simmering in both their hearts. She looked across at her companion to find him smiling casually at her. He sat with a glass of wine in his hand, totally at ease, as though it were

his custom to sit in her parlour in the early evening.
Collecting up the plates, she placed them on the tray.
To save Mrs Coleman the trouble of coming to remove
it, she picked it up and excused herself.

It was some minutes later when Catherine returned
and took her seat opposite John. Picking up her glass
of unfinished wine, she sipped it slowly. Relaxing
back in the comfortable upholstered chair, John felt
his heart soften as he gazed at her. He thought that it
was a crime for such loveliness to be hidden behind
closed doors. She was a vision. The firelight reflected
on the deep gold of her hair, which was drawn back
from her face with enchanting fluffy tendrils curling
on her cheeks. Her green eyes were luminous, her lips
tempting, her flesh soft. His fingers ached to caress it
as he had before. Catherine had no idea how intensely
he desired her.

Despite their angry words, he could not deny that
she had shown incredible bravery earlier. When she
had punched one of her assailants in the gut it had
not gone unnoticed by him. Looking at her now, her
long, incredible legs clad in breeches stretched out and
crossed at the ankles, who would have thought she was
a gently bred woman instructed in the manners and
deportment of a lady? She could have been mistaken
for a young gentleman, but the face, chiselled to perfection, was almost too beautiful to belong to a man.

'Did those ruffians hurt you?' he enquired. 'I'm
sorry, I should have asked before.'

'No, apart from my arm—a slight twist, but it is nothing.'

He watched her as she sipped her wine, contemplating the delight of taking her to bed again, removing her clothes and kissing those tempting lips and the bare flesh of her body. He loved her so much his heart ached with it.

'A woman alone is never safe. But you're a survivor. That's what I love about you.'

She forced a smile. 'Flatterer.'

'It's not flattery, Catherine.' His face was serious and there was an intensity in his eyes. A lock of hair had fallen across his brow and the firelight softened his angular face. 'You're a strange creature. Just as I think I'm getting to know you, some new trait shows itself. Take today, for instance. You showed no fear when those ruffians tried to steal your horse.'

'I was outraged that they even tried. But spare me from becoming predictable.'

'I doubt you will ever be that. And you are very beautiful.'

'What? Even in my breeches?' she remarked teasingly.

'Especially in your breeches. I find them very fetching.'

She sighed, shaking her head slowly and staring into the flames. 'I suppose life has taught me how to survive. I don't expect you to understand how I feel. In normal society there are few people who would understand me—what has made me like I am.'

'Do you think you are the only one to have suffered, Catherine?'

'No, of course I don't.'

'You accuse me of not understanding how you feel. There are few families that have been left untouched by tragedy. We all have burdens from the war.'

She looked at him steadily. 'Even you, John? Tell me.'

'You want there to be truth between us. I want that, too. No more secrets. The death of my older brother was just one of mine.'

'Just one?'

'No—my father killed himself—that was the other.' I should have told you all this before, but it is not something I am comfortable talking about.'

She stared at him, her beautiful eyes wide with shock at the abruptness of his statement. 'John— how—I am so sorry. I knew you had lost both your father and brother—I did not realise...'

'How could you?'

'Tell me.'

'My brother Richard was killed at the beginning of the war at Edgehill—which I have already told you. Father was a changed man afterwards—embittered. He did not respond to my mother, who thought the world of him. He threw himself into the war, determined to vent his anger on every Royalist who crossed his path. My mother lost not only her eldest son, but her husband also—even though he still lived. My brother was my father's shining light. The rest of his children did not compare. He missed him so much. He didn't want to live without him.

'I believe that when he rode into battle at Marston Moor, he wanted to die that day. When he became engaged in sword fight with a Royalist he could have won the fight and walked away, but he didn't. He didn't try. He stood and let the soldier strike him down and didn't raise his sword to defend himself.'

Catherine did not say anything, but simply sat there, listening as the words began pouring out of him. He spoke quietly about his painful past. She knew how hard it must be for him to say these things, each word uttered a word of pain. What she had been through was nothing compared to his suffering.

'I should not have been so quick to judge and you were right to chastise me.' John straightened and looked at her as if remembering she was there. His face looked haunted. 'You were there—at Marston Moor—and you saw it happen?'

'I did. I tried to save him—he spoke to me...'

'What did he say?'

'"Let me be." He died in my arms, but I don't believe he knew who I was.'

'That must have been very hard for you.'

'The hardest.'

Catherine saw tension in his face and heard the bitterness in his voice, and her heart wept for him. She felt that what had happened had affected him more deeply than even he realised.

'I never told anyone what happened that day. Moreover, I lost several friends in the debacle that was Marston Moor and found it hard to think about afterwards, let alone discuss what had happened.'

'That is understandable. I suppose no one who lived through that could ever be the same carefree person again.'

'That is true. I realised that I must take life seriously since I could never be sure that I wouldn't be plunged into a similar horror. I have never told anyone about my father. I have never discussed it, not even with my mother.'

'Perhaps it's kindest not to. There are some things a person is better off not knowing. Thank you for telling me, for sharing that with me.' She tilted her head to one side, her heart pounding so hard she believed he must hear it.

John got to his feet and crossed the room, lost in his thoughts. When he turned and came back to where she sat he looked down at her upturned face. 'Why are you going to Wilsden, Catherine? Are you running away?'

She thought about it and then nodded. 'I suppose I am in a way. There is nothing for me here. In fact, I don't want to be here any longer. This house—it's not my home any more. I don't even know a place I can call my home. Wilsden is the most dear, because it was where my mother grew up. The only drawback is that it's close to Carlton Bray.'

'What is it you want, Catherine?'

'That's simple—a home, hearth and contentment. Is that too much to ask?'

'Then marry me, Catherine. Marry me and let me take you to my home in Sussex. I know you will love it there.'

She stared up at him amazement. 'Marriage? But— but I had not thought...'

'You're not going to raise objections, are you? My nature, being what it is, I'll just ignore them. And please don't say this is all so sudden.'

'But, John, it is sudden...'

'I should have thought it was obvious, the way we were together—have you forgotten?'

'I forget nothing.'

'Thank goodness. I love you, Catherine. I admit it freely. No matter what you might say or do I—I know I will love you until the day I die. I cannot imagine my life without you. But for all that, I have no illusions about you. You are the most wilful, stubborn, temperamental woman I have ever known. There is much more—but above all else I want you to be my wife.' Taking her hand, he drew her up to stand before him.

'I—I don't know what to say.' She had spoken stiffly, but there was something in her eyes that made his heart beat wildly, a softness, a glowing. Was that love he saw in them?

'Answer me truthfully, John. Do you truly love me?'

'More than anything, my love—there will be nothing but the truth between us from now on. A thousand times or more I have cursed myself for a fool, but it would seem that I cannot help loving you. I want you to marry me—be my wife, bear my children and live a happy life.' He gazed at her for a long moment, then moved closer. Raising his hand, he brushed a stray curl from her face with his fingertip. 'Harbour no more thoughts of running away, Catherine. I'm not so easily got rid of. You remember how it was between us when we spent the night together beneath this very roof. It can be like that again—every night of our lives, if you want it to be. Marry me, Catherine.'

Catherine stared at him. 'Yes, yes I will,' she answered. 'How could I ever forget what it was like when we were together? It was the most wonderful thing that has happened to me in my life. But there is one thing you should know—something I have to tell you.'

'And what is that?'

'I am with child, John. Your child.'

John's eyes opened wide with astonishment, then his face became thoughtful, his eyes narrowed speculatively. 'A child? Good Lord!' He had not expected this, but he should have known it was a possibility when he took her to bed. 'How long have you known?'

'A few days,' she murmured, half turning her head away. 'At first I wasn't sure, having no experience of such things, but now I am as certain as I can be.'

He stood straight, moving a step away from her, his face impassive—the expression he normally used to shield his thoughts when troubled or angry. A muscle began to twitch in his cheek. He stared down at her, his face expressing bewilderment, disbelief and finally agony as the realisation of what she had intended dawned on him. After what seemed like a lifetime later, he turned her face to his, forcing her to look at him, his eyes hard and intense.

'When were you going to tell me?' he demanded. 'When, Catherine?'

He continued to fix her with his gaze, demanding an answer. Catherine shook her head, turning her face away once more, as if she couldn't bear to look at him. He took her chin in his fingers and forced her to face him, her eyes full of mournful sadness.

'Look at me, Catherine. Come—tell me the truth. What did you intend by keeping such an important matter from me? Was it some kind of test you were putting me through? A test of my love?' He shook his head slowly, in disbelief and disappointment when she didn't answer. 'Oh, Catherine—I think you take your independence too far. What if I hadn't come across you today in London? What would you have done? Would you have gone to Wilsden tomorrow and let me live out my life ignorant of the fact that I had a child somewhere?'

When she refused to answer, in his outrage John flung himself away from her, unable to believe she would have done anything as cruel as that. Then, with a calm, business like manner he strode to the door.

'John—where are you going? You can't leave me like this…'

'I'm going out. You'll find out where when I return shortly. You must understand that I had a right to know about this. From now on we shall make any decisions regarding our child together. Is that understood, Catherine?'

* * *

An hour later when John had not returned, Catherine went to her bedchamber, tired and despondent, with the intention of going to bed. She was wrapped in her robe when he walked in, having escaped the watchful eyes of Mrs Coleman. Catherine's face was pale and tense, evidence of the nervous strain she had been under since his departure. She had no idea where he had gone to in such a hurry or if he would return. She only knew that she had never felt so miserable before in her life. She had been foolish to think she could keep a matter of such importance from him—not that she would have done. Had she gone to Wilsden, she would have written to him, telling him about the child, hoping he would come to her.

When he entered she hurried to him. 'John, where have you been? I thought you weren't coming back.'

'Of course I was coming back. Since we are to have a child together then I have a responsibility to both you and the child. I've been to pay a call on the minister of your local church to arrange our wedding.'

Catherine's eyes opened wide in astonishment. 'Wedding?'

He smiled down at her. 'We are getting married in two days' time. You will marry me, won't you, Catherine?'

Catherine flung herself into his arms, not knowing whether to laugh or cry with happiness. 'I've already said yes,' she said softly. 'You don't know how happy that makes me.' She leaned back in his arms and looked at him. 'I'm glad it will be soon.'

'I love you so much. I do want you—with or without a child—although knowing you carry my child makes me extremely happy. And it's no good thinking you can flee to Wilsden. I would come after you. It's no good fighting me, you should know that by now. I will have you one way or another.'

Placing his hands on her shoulders, he drew her close, kissing her lips tenderly. 'Much as I would like to, I can't stay. There's much to be done in the coming days. Hopefully the King's trial won't last long. Afterwards I will leave the army and go to Sussex. We will go there together—as husband and wife.'

'I ask for nothing more. I'm sorry you have to leave tonight.'

'So am I.' With a final kiss he left her.

John and Catherine were married in the same church where her parents were buried in the church yard. The ceremony was brief. Apart from two of John's fellow soldiers, Mrs Coleman and a few servants from Oakdene House, there were no other guests. There had been no time to inform John's mother of the wedding, but he intended taking Catherine down to Sussex very soon. They made their vows to each other. John's heart was full of love as he looked at his bride and Catherine was so overcome with emotion and love that she wept.

When they were declared to be man and wife, John took Catherine in his arms and held her close. 'You are mine at last, Catherine, and legally bound. There was never a more beautiful bride.' He smiled suddenly. 'Your status has been elevated to Countess, too, my love. You are now Countess Fitzroy of Inglewood in Sussex.'

Catherine's eyes opened wide. 'Goodness, I had not thought about it—although I know I should. How grand it sounds.'

'And deserving.'

Afterwards they returned to Oakdene, where Mrs Coleman had laid out a spread fit for a king. When everyone had eaten their fill, raised their glasses in toasts to a happy and fruitful marriage, Catherine and John found themselves alone at last.

John watched his wife as she prepared for bed. She was both exquisite and unforgettable. She was utterly irresistible and he felt his bones melt when he saw the soft flush in her cheeks, the gentle curve of her neck, the stubborn tilt of her chin, the way her body swayed when she walked across a room, vibrant and strong. He found himself wanting to kiss her senseless, to feel her melt in his arms, to taste those lips once more. Heat burned in his blood. This was madness. Why was Catherine different from any other woman he had known? Why did he feel different? Why was he tormenting himself like this when she was his for the taking?

He smiled at her. 'You have a peculiar look in your

eyes, my love,' he murmured. 'One would think you were in an amorous mood.'

'Well, considering this is my wedding night, perhaps I am,' she replied, settling herself more comfortably on the bed.

'Would you like to do something about it? It could be arranged,' he said in suggestive tones.

'Then perhaps you should.' Getting off the bed, she padded across to him and, reaching up, she drew his head down to hers and kissed his lips. Of their own volition her fingers curved around his neck, sliding into the soft, thick hair at his nape.

'Tonight we have all the time in the world to enjoy each other and I don't intend to waste one minute of it.'

As he spoke he unbound her hair, letting the curls cascade to her shoulders. As her hands slid over his chest, she felt the strong grip of his arms and his warm mouth was on hers. In the darkness outside, the screech of an owl could be heard as it soared into the sky. There was nothing that was needed in her chamber, only the two of them who had waited so long for this night, impatient for each other. No words were needed for the present—there would be time for that later.

The very air bristled with the energy sparking between them. Neither of them tried to conquer their desire. The attraction between them had been denied too long. Catherine realised how tight her nipples had grown. Her body was ripe for his teasing lips. He slid the gown over her shoulders, letting the fabric drop until it caught at her waist. His hands caressed her bare flesh, rosy in the fire's glow, cupping each breast, his fingers provoking their taut pink crowns and forcing a shameless moan from her throat before they slid down her sides, stopping at the swell of her hips where the gown still clung. With an impatient tug at its fastenings, the gown instantly dropped to her feet. His hands stroked the curve of her spine and her blood surged in eager response, until she was consumed with a need that mirrored his own. Her skin tingled where he touched it, sending quivers through the depths of her.

She was beautiful, utterly so. His eyes caressed every curve of her body, every indentation of her skin. He kissed her lightly along the slender column of her throat, trailing his lips down between the luscious swells of her naked breasts, twin mounds of perfection swollen with the ache of desire. The moment Catherine felt his arms about her, her naked body caught against the hard pressure of his manhood, her passion blazed. He kissed her throat, her cheeks, her mouth, until she forgot everything and, when they tumbled down on to the bed, she prepared to abandon herself to him completely. Her skin warmed with colour and, unable to resist him, eyes closed, she kissed him as ardently as he kissed her.

His love play was agonisingly subtle and delicious, teasing her desire to the limits of endurance, feeling her writhing and panting under his touch as warm breasts, firm thighs and moist lips moulded themselves to his body. He touched her everywhere, as though to assert his possessive entitlement to every inch of her.

Her neck arched backwards, eyes half-closed, her lips partly open, for the second time in her life, Catherine was experiencing heaven. Her heart beat in her ears like thunder, her excitement mounted uncontrollably and she wanted him to take her immediately.

His experienced, accomplished hands and lips drew nearer to her trembling thighs. As she writhed in intolerable bliss, they parted. Fiercely she held him to her, trying to get as close to him as she could. She watched his expression changing, making him unbelievably beautiful and sending her emotions even higher. Giving herself up to total abandon, she arced her body in hot impatience, trembling for him in frantic yearning. She had never needed anything more than this man inside her now.

He wrapped his arms more firmly around her. Cradling her body to him, he pressed a kiss to her brow and took her with skilled seduction. Never had she imagined there was such intoxicating pleasure to be had from surrendering utterly. His dark hair was tousled. Stormy passion lit his eyes, so that they glowed as he made love to her in earnest, transporting her to new heights. He gave with determined vigour as she soared and hurtled through a heaven of sensations that exploded through her.

And then there came release.

'I love you,' John murmured, then kissed her cheek with such tenderness.

'And I love you, John. More than you will ever know. Never doubt it.'

He didn't move away and she held him in her arms, cradling his head on her chest in the lingering amazement of their joining. She had never experienced anything like the tangible bond their lovemaking had wrought. For the first time in her life she felt free and believed she would be happy. She was loved by John, more deeply, more tenderly than she had ever believed possible.

Catherine had fallen asleep, having relished every driving thrust of her husband's body against hers, bringing her to peak after peak of every emotion she was capable of. Everything that had happened to her seemed like a wonderful dream. On waking, at first she looked about her, unable to remember where she was or what she was doing here, lying naked in bed with a man beside her, his arms holding her close, the light streaming in through the windows and throwing every detail of their bodies in relief.

She must have moved, or perhaps it was only her suddenly quickened breathing that had aroused him. She felt his arms tighten and his lips brushed her forehead.

'Good morning, my dear wife,' he murmured, his warm lips nuzzling her ear. 'Did you sleep well?'

Catherine met his eyes, heavy-lidded still from his slumber, and he gave her a lazy grin. She smiled back. 'Well enough,' she replied. 'Considering it was an eventful night and you allowed me little sleep.' He laughed throatily and she realised what a lovely sound it was.

'As I recall, you gave me little chance of falling asleep myself. It would appear I have married a wanton—not that I'm complaining, my love,' he said, capturing her mouth in a kiss that was both searching and tender, leaving Catherine hungry for more. Releasing her lips and trailing his own down the column of her throat, pausing to caress the area where a pulse beat hard beneath her flesh, he murmured, 'It is a side to your nature I welcome. Neither of us will be bored in our marriage—quite the opposite, in fact.'

'And you, my lord, have turned out to be a man with many conflicting sides to your character.'

'How so?' His mouth continued to trail a path to her breasts.

'Why, one minute you are like a ravenous wolf, then next a tender and considerate lover.'

'And which do you prefer? The wolf or the lamb?'

She sighed, closing her eyes and letting him have his way. At that moment, lying in his arms in the warm cocoon of the bed, she didn't want to think. Her body craved the erotic sensations he had aroused in her last night. Having learned the meaning of desire and fulfilment, she wanted to be transported out of herself, reassure herself that such sensations actually existed. He had learned the secrets of her body and she his. They had both learned what pleased the other, what kind of caresses they enjoyed. When she shifted her body better to accommodate him, he paused and captured her eyes.

'What?' he asked.

She smiled, bringing his head down to hers. 'Don't stop now,' she whispered. 'Not when I'm about to enjoy what you do to me all over again.'

Epilogue

The savage mockery of a trial was over at last. The King of England had been condemned to death. At almost two o'clock on January the thirtieth 1649, he stepped on to the scaffold which had been erected outside the Banqueting House in Whitehall. A groan went up from the onlookers as his head was separated from his body.

John looked away. It was a day to remember for ever—the day when Englishmen murdered their King.

There were those present who muttered, 'God save King Charles the Second,' little knowing that the young King Charles would have many years as a hunted man, with nothing ahead of him but the dark days of a fugitive.

Catherine did not go into the city for the execution. She had no wish to witness a man's violent death, least of all a king's.

Just one week later, Catherine and John travelled to Sussex, to his home and now her home, Inglewood

House, in a landscape that was varied and beautiful and just two miles from the towering chalk cliffs overlooking the English Channel.

Inglewood House was a welcoming, red-brick mansion at the end of a tree-lined approach, the bricks having mellowed since it was built a century earlier. Built in pleasing symmetry, it stood in perfect harmony against a backdrop of woods and well-cultivated farmland. Around the house were gardens heavily planted with laurel and flowers, and tall oak trees overshadowing ponds where in the summer water lilies would strive to bloom in the gentle shade.

'It's a beautiful house,' Catherine murmured on the approach. 'It's just as I expected it to be.'

'I know you'll like it here, Catherine. It's a peaceful place—quiet, too, except for the harvest when the workers take to the fields and often raise their voices in song as they labour, and when the bells toll from the village church. My mother and Elizabeth cannot wait to meet you before they go to Kent to stay with my brother Stephen and his family. When Blanche leaves for Carlton Bray we'll have the house to ourselves.'

'I do so hope your mother and sister aren't leaving on my account.'

'No. It's a visit long promised.'

Margaret, Dowager Countess Fitzroy, John's mother, came out of the parlour to welcome them as soon as they arrived. She was closely followed by a young woman with dark hair and a smile stretched wide on her pretty face.

The years had not been kind to the Dowager. Her hair was grey, her once attractive face lined with past anxieties, but her eyes were sharp and intelligent and warm. John covered the distance between them and gathered her into his arms.

'Mother, how are you?'

'I am much better and relieved to have you home at last—to stay, I hope.'

'I am—and, Elizabeth,' he said, embracing his sister. 'Why, look at you. You've grown at least a foot since I last saw you.'

'Yes, John,' she replied, unable to conceal the adoration she felt for her older brother. Her gaze went to Catherine, hovering several yards away.

John went to her. 'There is someone I would like you to meet.' Taking Catherine's hand, he drew her forward. 'Mother, Elizabeth, I would like to introduce you to Catherine, my wife and soon-to-be mother of my child.'

Catherine sank into a curtsy. With tears in her eyes, the Dowager embraced Catherine before holding her at arm's length and studying her closely. 'Welcome to Inglewood. You have no idea how long I have waited for this day. I am well pleased that you and John are married. It's time he settled down. You are very lovely, my dear—although John did write telling us of your marriage. Which, I might add,' she said, glancing at her son with mock reproach, 'was one of the few letters I have received from him while he's been away.'

'I never was one for letter writing, Mother, as well you know.'

'I do—just a few lines scrawled on a piece of paper had to suffice. If what he has told us is true, Catherine, you are a remarkable young woman who defended Carlton Bray Castle on your own against hostile forces during the war.'

Catherine flushed. 'I think your son exaggerates, Lady Margaret—not entirely on my own.'

'Nevertheless, you were in an unenviable position and you acted bravely. I am proud to have you as my daughter-in-law. I know we are going to be great friends. Now come into the parlour. I am sure you would like some refreshment after your journey.'

As they partook of refreshment, listening to the constant chatter between the Dowager and Elizabeth and John, Catherine had to swallow down a lump in her throat and blink away tears in her eyes. She was unable to remember the last time she had sat with a family which was a normal everyday occurrence for most people, but it had not been for her. Not since her own mother had died. John's mother and sister were prepared to accept her unconditionally and for that she would be eternally gratefully.

'Where is Blanche?' she asked tentatively.

'She's taken James into the garden. She's expecting you and will be in shortly. I have to say James is such a lovely little boy. We're going to miss him when she takes him to Carlton Bray.'

* * *

Blanche received Catherine with surprising warmth. She looked relaxed and happy. Catherine returned her smile with a lifting of her heart. Perhaps it was right that time healed the wounds of the past.

The following morning, with James scampering on ahead of them, they strolled together in the wintery garden, down the walks that in summer would be a blazing riot of flowers.

'This is a lovely house, don't you think, Blanche?'

'Yes, and the garden. You are so fortunate to be living here, Catherine. The sea is close. We took James to the beach. He loved it.'

'John has told you about his plans for Carlton Bray, Blanche. Does the idea of living there please you?'

'I could not be happier. I never expected him to do that. It is a generous offer and I appreciate it so much.'

'It must be a satisfaction for you.'

'Yes. I can't tell you what that means to me, that James will inherit the estate some time in the future and pass it on to his descendants—when all the politics have been worked out. He will get to know his father there.'

'He will have you to tell him.' Catherine smiled. 'It's strange, isn't it, that I was Thomas's wife and yet I didn't know him at all. I'm sure you'll be happy there—although Carlton Bray is far removed from London. It's very quiet—but the people of Carlton

village have always been loyal to the Stratton family.
I know they'll welcome you both.'

'That is what I hope. And you, Catherine—you are
to live here in Sussex. Will you sell Oakdene?'

'No—at least, not yet. It's early days. For the present
I've decided to rent it out. I've instructed my lawyer
to look for someone. I'm sure there is someone who
would like to live there.'

'Yes, there will be. I hope they will be happier than
I was. You know, Catherine, you are fortunate in your
husband. I did have designs on him myself. I think
I saw him as the father James has never had and he
would be my link to Thomas. John is an attractive man,
but I saw in which direction his attraction lay when he
brought you back to Oakdene.'

'You did?'

'I'm not blind, Catherine. But see—everything has
turned out splendidly.'

Living at Inglewood House, Catherine came to the
realisation that she had never been happier in her life.
When the weather improved, Lady Margaret and Elizabeth left for Kent for an extended visit with John's
youngest brother and his family. An excited Blanche
and James left for the Welsh Marches with an escort
provided by John. After several weeks she wrote that
she and James had settled at Carlton Bray very well
and how helpful Will Price was to her. In fact, she
even went as far as to indicate that she would be very
sorry should John decide to recall him. On reading this

John and Catherine looked at each other with raised eyebrows and then very slowly they smiled when they realised what this might mean. Was it possible that Blanche and Will were attracted to one another?

'You will leave him there, won't you, John?'

'Will is free to do as he wants, my love. If staying at Carlton Bray with Blanche and James is what he wants to do, then so be it. Although how he will withstand living in Thomas's shadow remains to be seen.'

Catherine had settled down to life at Inglewood with remarkable ease. It was like being enfolded in affectionate, warm and willing arms. It was like a dream, a rainbow-coloured dream. But here was John, reminding her that it was actually happening after all and that all those unpleasant events of the past had happened to someone else.

Their son came into the world in late summer. Named William Henry Stratton, he was a lusty boy who was adored and spoiled by all. John was a proud father. On the child's birth he had taken the small bundle in his arms as his wife looked on with a deep and abiding love in her eyes. After a moment he raised his eyes to hers.

'I told my mother when I married you that you are a remarkable woman, Catherine. I did not exaggerate.'

His compliment brought a flush to her face. It touched her heart to have him looking at her so, as if she had accomplished some great deed—which he assured her she had. She wanted to live every moment of what the future brought to the full. But for now, she would live this moment, this wonderful moment, and savour the joy of loving and being loved.

'Thank you,' he said, the soft tones of his voice warming her as she gazed into his eyes.

Catherine felt herself being drawn into his gaze and she couldn't miss the approval in the tender smile he gave her. 'It was my pleasure,' she replied, reaching out and caressing the curly-headed infant in his arms. 'I love you. I shall love you until the day I die, John Stratton. Promise me that nothing shall ever come between us.' She put up a finger and traced the line of his jaw.

'I do. I promise.'

* * * * *

If you enjoyed this story, why not check out these other great reads by Helen Dickson

Carrying the Gentleman's Secret
A Vow for an Heiress
The Governess's Scandalous Marriage
Reunited at the King's Court
Wedded for His Secret Child